like a woman

like a woman

debra busman

DZANC
BOOKS

DZANC BOOKS

5220 Dexter Ann Arbor Rd.
Ann Arbor, MI 48103
www.dzancbooks.org

Cover art by Oscar Hernandez
Designed by Steven Seighman

Library of Congress Cataloging-in-Publication Data

Busman, Debra, 1953-
  Like a Woman : a novel / by Debra Busman.
      pages cm
  1. Teenage girls—Fiction. 2. Self-realization—Fiction. 3. Los Angeles (Calif.)—Fiction. 4. Bildungsromans. I. Title.
  PS3602.U8446L55 2014
  813'.6—dc23

                                        2014013392

ISBN: 978-1-938103-24-7

First U.S. Edition: March 2015

Printed in the United States of America

10   9   8   7   6   5   4   3   2   1

Contents

PART ONE

A Fire that Had to Burn

The Book of Bad Men

The first job Taylor ever had was pulling down her pants and peeing in front of the old man who lived in the wash behind the Hollywood Freeway. It was easy money. Steady work. Flexible hours. He never touched her, never frightened her. Just gave her dimes for every puddle she made. She was seven.

At first she used the money to buy sodas and ice cream. Then she figured out that having just a little money made it so much easier to steal. She could walk into a store like she belonged, strut up to the counter with her two extra-large cans of Alpo dog food, and hand over the money, all in dimes. Twenty-nine cents. Three puddles' worth, with a penny back. The checkout lady would say, "Oh, how sweet. Do you have a doggy, little girl?" and she would answer, "Yes ma'am," and smile at the cool, scratchy feel of the Gaines Burger packets stuffed up under her shirt, pressed tight against her flat chest, back and belly.

Taylor fed all the stray dogs and cats in the neighborhood. That was her other job, but of course that one didn't pay. Hollering for the Shepherd/Collie mix with the hurt foot was how she had first met the man in the wash. She'd called the dog Shane until she found out he was a girl dog and then she called her Shane anyway. The old guy said he'd seen the dog earlier that morning and helped Taylor look for her. They got to talking about dogs and pretty soon the guy was telling Taylor about every dog he'd ever had since he was a little boy—Blue Tick hounds, Chocolate Labs, a little Terrier named Snitch, and even a purebred Dalmatian fire engine dog.

When Taylor said she had to go back home, the old man said, "Why? It's still early," and she said, "Because I gotta pee," and he said, "That ain't no reason to leave, honey. You can just squat right here in the sand. That's how Shane would do it, isn't it, honey?" And she thought about it and he was right, that was how Shane would do it, and why should she waste time running back home.

Taylor pulled down her jeans and underpants, squatted and peed, careful to not let the hot liquid touch her legs or shoes. She watched the sand turn dark as the puddle spread. It felt good, very liberating, like she'd discovered something the other kids didn't know—that you didn't have to go inside and use a bathroom if you needed to pee, not even if you were a girl. Then the old guy gave her a dime and said, "Now this will be our little secret, won't it," and she nodded, zipping up her pants. Taylor understood about secrets.

The trouble started one day when Taylor was running out of the house, bladder full, to look for Shane and the old man. "Where you going and where'd you get that book?" her mama yelled after her, stopping the girl in her tracks. Taylor looked down at the *Encyclopedia of Dogs* she had stolen from the five and dime.

"Never steal, unless it's from the government," her mom always said with a laugh but with eyes that meant business.

"It's my dog book," Taylor said, turning around slowly. "I got it from a friend."

"What friend?" her mom laughed. "You don't have any friends that can read."

Truth was, Taylor didn't have any friends at all yet in the new neighborhood, but now she was backed into a corner. "Do so." She clutched the book to her chest. "I got a friend who lives over by the freeway."

Taylor never figured out quite how her world unraveled so fast. First her mom got all red and angry, interrogating her about the man in the wash—who was he and how did she know him and what did he do to her and did he touch her, did he touch her, did he touch her? "No, Mama. He don't never touch me. We just talk about dogs. He's my friend." And did he ever touch her and did he ever make her touch him and did he ever touch her *down there?* "Mama, I told you, he don't never touch me and I ain't never touched him. He's my friend and he gives me dimes when I pee and we talk about dogs and he helps me feed Shane..." And then it was over.

The next thing she knew there were police everywhere. Three of them were right inside her house, two plainclothes from a squad car and one motorcycle cop standing by the door, arms crossed, sunglasses and helmet still on. Taylor started to tremble. She knew her mom was terrified of cops, hated 'em worse than head lice and Satan, but there she was talking to them like there was something in the world even worse than cops and Taylor hadn't yet known that such a thing existed.

"Here, honey," the older cop said. "We'd just like you to take a look in this book and tell us if you see the man who hurt you. These are all pictures of bad men. Tell us if you see anyone who looks like the man who hurt you."

Taylor stared at the huge brown book lying open on the table in front of her. Rows and rows of black-and-white mugshots blurred before her eyes. She counted the men, six across, seven rows down, the plastic-covered pages yellowed, peeling, and worn.

"But he didn't hurt me," she said, her voice thin and soft.

"Now tell us just exactly what he did to you," the cop continued. "Did he touch you? Did he make you touch him? Did he put his fingers where they didn't belong? Did he touch your privates? Did he touch, you know, your pee hole?"

Taylor felt like she was going to throw up. She had never been so close to a cop before. She looked down at the table where he was still touching the book. His hand was huge, the knuckles covered with dark hair, furry, just like her uncle's hand. Her uncle touched her down there. His hands had touched her pee hole. His thick fingers had pressed against her lips. It was a secret.

Taylor wondered if her uncle's picture was in the brown book. She looked up at the motorcycle cop standing by the door. She wondered what he was smiling at. She thought he looked like a shiny black insect. She wanted to run for the door but she knew he would grab her if she tried. Then the older cop put his hand on her shoulder and she screamed. The hot piss ran down her legs, steaming into her socks.

as a child i believed

as a child i believed we came from wolves, somehow lost, separated inside the city's mass. the children, that is. i had no idea where adults came from, but i thought that children were all adopted, picked out like puppies from the pound. some got good homes with lots of food and room to play. some could only cower at the boot, snarl, or run away to try again. my home was not particularly good, except that it was filled with other strays, the pain came mostly in the night, and there was enough to eat.

in that schoolyard moment when the other kids informed me that we didn't come from wolves, several strands were broken from the fraying thread that held me to that place and time. i was actually quite shocked by their versions of how we came to be in families. i never spoke of it again, but secretly, i still dreamed about the wolves. i'd hear the special howl the wolves used to bring their children home, and i'd run to join them. we'd all tumble together with lots of suckling, wrestling and chewing on ears. licked and growling, nuzzled about, tufts of fur in happy mouths, coming up for air.

Like the Wind

Taylor's favorite job was stealing from Sears, working for her best friend Mario's uncle Enrique. Enrique had hated Sears ever since he'd gotten fired for pointing out to management that the tan blond workers seemed to be having way too much fun while the brown workers got all the shit jobs and early pink slips. So Sears was the usual target of choice, although Pep Boys and Montgomery Wards were also fair game. Taylor stole bicycles, clothes, electronics, tools, watches—anything she could grab and ride or run away with.

She and Mario had figured out pretty quick that, as a nine-year-old white girl, Taylor wasn't followed around by security cops like her Mexican friends. So the kids would all separate before entering a store, Mario, Jesus, and Ricky going in one door and Taylor in the other, her hair combed, her pink blouse clean and pressed. Once inside, Jesus and Mario would start a fight, or Ricky would "get lost" and cry for his mama, or they would "accidentally" knock down the five-foot-high pyramid of Valvoline 10-40 motor oil cans. Once personnel went running to investigate the commotion, Taylor stuffed something in her jacket or, when she was lucky, hopped on a ten-speed or Sting Ray bike and just rode right out the door. "Like the wind," Enrique would say. "That girl rides like the motherfuckin' wind."

All she had to do was ride down the street until she saw Enrique's white van. If all was clear, he'd open the back doors and throw Taylor and the bike inside. If someone was after her, Enrique left the van doors shut, looked away, and she'd know to keep on riding, ditch the bike and start hopping fences. They never once got caught, although Taylor hopped a lot of fences.

Once inside the van, she and Enrique circled around to the other side of the shopping center to pick up Mario, Jesus, and Ricky down by whatever gas station they'd checked out beforehand, usually a Chevron or a Union 76, because Ricky liked the little orange balls they gave away. The boys would all pile in and brag about what they'd done to attract security and everyone would laugh. Taylor would tell them how she got away, and then Enrique would say, "Damn, you guys done good," and tousle their hair. Then he'd light up a reefer for him and Mario to smoke and sometimes Taylor took a hit, too.

Taylor had that job until she turned thirteen and Enrique got drafted. Four years and she never called in sick, never missed a day of work. Enrique was an excellent boss. He taught Taylor tricks that would serve her throughout her life. Like never *act* like you're stealing when you're stealing. Act like you already own it, like it already belongs to you and somehow got misplaced on the shelf by mistake. "Ride that motherfuckin' bike like it's *yours*, girl," he used to tell Taylor. "Not like you're stealing it from no goddamn pussy Sears store."

Sometimes, Taylor got to see Enrique in action himself. Once, when his grandmother needed a new refrigerator, he brought home a brand-new Westinghouse double-door chrome handle with deluxe icemaker. First, he stole a pair of overalls from Sears that looked just like the ones the guys wore down at the Montgomery Wards warehouse. Then he sewed on a nametag—"Frankie," he laughed.

"Es un buen nombre, no?" Taylor watched Enrique check out the appliance section of the Van Nuys Wards a couple of times and then damn if he didn't just walk right into the store and come out the back a few minutes later wheeling a huge, shiny refrigerator on a bright red dolly. Stole the dolly, too.

Every time Enrique would tell the story of how he stole his grandmother's refrigerator he'd just laugh and say, "Ah sí, mi abuelita. We never did find out how el refrigerador de mi abuelita wound up at Montgomery Wards. Qué misterio!" He'd smile, his eyes crinkling up. "Pues," he'd continue. "Once I knew the refrigerator was in the wrong place, I had to liberate it, no? Bring it back to my grandmother where it belonged. It's only right, you know. Es la verdad."

Enrique was shot two months after being shipped out to Nam. Killed by friendly fire while he was out taking a piss, two days after his battalion finally got their ammo and were heading for the front lines. He never stopped talking to Taylor, though. Every time she stole a bike, she'd hear his voice whispering in her ear. "*Ride* that bike like the motherfuckin' wind. Ride it like it's yours." When she'd walk into a bookstore, Taylor could hear Enrique's voice get real low and fierce. "Yes, chica," she'd hear him say, "these books *belong* to you. Liberate one or two for me while you're at it. And, remember to share them with los niños, okay? *Some*one's got to redistribute the wealth, eh mija?"

Even as Taylor got older, Enrique was still right there with helpful advice. "Look like you belong," he told her when she started stealing from the fancy department stores downtown, "*especially* if you don't." When her clothes got too shabby, he warned her, "Niña, te acuerdas, only the rich can afford to dress poor." In fact, it was Enrique's idea to start selling raggedy jeans to the hippies out in Griffith Park. Taylor and Mario collected worn out Levi's and work shirts from all the neighbors, pulling them from the hands of the mothers who first wanted to sew up the tears in their son's, brother's, husband's clothes.

"No, Mama," Mario would say. "That's the whole point. You don't gotta sew this shit anymore. Taylor's gonna sell 'em to los hippies. They pay *more* money if the pants are torn. I *know* que está muy loco, Mama, pero es la verdad. Give them to me. You'll see."

Every Saturday, Taylor and Mario took the bus down to Griffith Park and sold the raggedy clothes to the hippies at their love-ins and anti-war rallies. Taylor was dealing pot to them anyway, so it was pretty easy to set up shop. In fact, it was a great cover and explained any money Taylor might have on her if the cops rousted them. Mario stood out too much in the crowd, so he stayed clean, laid low, and watched, ready to cover Taylor's back if necessary. Every weekend, they brought home more money, and every Monday the women in the neighborhood went out to Sears to buy new jeans for their kids, new work shirts for their husbands.

One day, as they watched the kids head off to school in their brand-new clothes, Mario leaned up against Taylor. "Hey, *only the rich can afford to dress poor*, right?" he whispered.

Taylor looked at him, surprised. "Where'd you hear that?"

Mario laughed. "Hey man, you don't think you're the only one he talks to, do you? That motherfucker's been yappin' inside my head ever since he got shot. That cholo talks more now than when he was alive."

Taylor shook her head. "No kiddin'?" she asked. "He ever sing that stupid-ass Dylan song to you?"

"Oh man," Mario whined. "Only all the fucking time. Every time I even think about shaking somebody down or putting some of the hippie money in my own pocket, I gotta hear that guy singing, *to leeve out side the law, chu mus be ho-nest...*"

Taylor laughed. She'd heard that refrain on more than one occasion herself. "Come on," she said, pushing Mario gently. "Let's go check out what those motherfuckers got on sale today down at Sears. Hey, *somebody's* got to redistribute the wealth. Right?"

death was just a fence away

it was in the place they had not paved that i spent most of my time. down in the hot, sandy wash, beyond the city park, filled with rocks and bottles, old abandoned shells of cars and men, where kids and lizards scurried, and the rest moved kind of slow. where i brought crumpled bits of lettuce to feed my neighbor's tortoise hidden in the brush. (it ran away! i said, with eyes as big as lies. the truth was i couldn't stand to see it poked, and when i read that turtles hate to have you even touch their shell, my body shivered with familiarity and i did what a child must do.)

once, as i fed the tortoise's old man mouth and watched its blinky eyes, i felt something else watching me, and turned up to face an exploding sun surrounding the huge gila monster i would come to know as friend. the new creature slowly backed into its ledge, and it took me months of sweaty practice to cease my rude and human stare that frightened all things wild. lying belly down in the hot, gravelly sand, in time i learned to soften focus, and soon my presence caused little more than a raised reptilian eyelid, and i could lie down nose to nose with the ancient gritty ones and ask them anything i wanted in a time both safe and slow.

when the men arrived to put the freeway in, time shifted irrevocably. i could not find the wise, scaly friends that kept me in this world, and i wandered, my spirit broken as a bulldozed tortoise shell. i learned again to harden focus, glare out my intent, and never move too slow. and as i watched the freeway cars race by, sometimes held inside their cyclone cages, i noticed how the screaming sirens passed more quickly than they arrived, and i found my adolescent comfort knowing death was just a fence away.

The Story of David

All she wanted was to get a look inside that open casket and see if David really was in there. Before he died, he had lived next door. He'd been hit by a car when he was seven but that wasn't what killed him. Last week Taylor had seen the medics wheel something out of the house. The ambulance had screeched up fast and loud, then crawled away slow, its sirens silent. Still, she needed to see for herself if the boy was in that box.

Taylor sat up in the front pew with David's family, the Doyles, sweating and squirming in her itchy yellow church dress, the dingy, permanently starched ruffles grating into her neck. She didn't think you were supposed to wear yellow to funerals but she only had one church dress and her mom said God didn't care what color her dress was.

"Well, if he don't care what color my dress is, then why should he care if I even wear a dress at all?" Taylor had asked, neither expecting nor receiving a reply. She hated dresses. She hated God. And she hated church. Unfortunately they all went together; plus now she had a hundred-degree day, a pee-leaking baby—David's little brother Bobby—on her lap, and an old man in a robe talking forever about Purgatory, captive souls, deliverance, and damnation.

Taylor felt Mike, the oldest of the six Doyle boys, nudge her shoulder. "Okay, we're gonna go look at him now."

"What about the baby? He ain't supposed to see, is he?" Taylor whispered. She looked over at Mike's mom, sitting with her newly dyed black hair pulled back tight, staring out the crucified Jesus stained-glass window. Mrs. Doyle's hands gripped together in her lap, the fingernails all cut short except on the baby fingers where the slightly yellow nails curled long and crooked. Taylor shivered slightly, pulled the baby closer. Mr. Doyle sat next to his wife, alternately holding her elbow and wiping his palms on his pants, pulling at his tight white collar and looking for the door. He was a tall, thick man who moved slow and didn't talk much but could whip off his belt quicker than you could spit. Kids usually stayed out of his way.

"I don't know," Mike said. "I guess you hold him while I look and I'll hold him while you look." The borrowed grey suit hung loose on Mike's skinny frame. The pants were cinched up tight, revealing dark mismatched socks and his father's stiff black shoes. At thirteen, he was still waiting to grow into his ears, which looked even larger than usual with his new buzz haircut.

"Okay," said Taylor. "I'll hold him first. But watch out, he's pretty wet." She and Mike stood up, joining the slow-moving procession past the open coffin. Tommy, the next oldest, came with them, leaving the nine- and six-year-olds, Ryan and Sean, sitting stiffly on the bench by themselves, leaning like a couple of bowling pins left after a missed strike. Nobody moved to fill in the gap. Across the aisle, their neighbor Mrs. Jablonski gave a slight tsking sound, gathered up her girth and took the leaking baby from Taylor. Making her way over to the two boys, Mrs. Jablonski plumped herself down next to Sean. Taylor was relieved that the scent of rotting rose petals left with her.

Waiting for the line to move, Taylor watched Sean squint sideways up at the big lady holding his baby brother and squishing him up against Ryan. Taylor couldn't remember ever having seen Mrs. Jablonski without her hair curlers in. Blond at the ends, her hair turned into an orangey black up close to the scalp, reminding Taylor of David's favorite marble. She held back a smile as Sean wrinkled his nose and looked down at Mrs. Jablonski's legs, straining against the damp floral dress, forcing her knees far apart. Each thigh was bigger around than the whole of Sean's body. Taylor watched Sean look down at his own legs, skinny and straight, knees touching easily. He bounced them together a few times, glanced over at Bobby asleep in between the folds of Mrs. Jablonski's stomach and breasts, and then closed his eyes. Bobby snored softly.

Tommy, Mike, and Taylor moved up the line, closer to the open casket.

"He looks like somebody colored his face all up with crayons," whispered Tommy. Taylor peered in at David's white, waxy body, lying stretched out straight, hands to his side, dressed in a Navy blue Goodwill suit. She'd seen enough animals die to know that bodies look different without their souls, and her mom had warned her that David wouldn't really be "there" in the box. Still, she hated to see him this way: head sculptured, lips painted, scars covered, body straightened out into the narrow child coffin. She longed to carry him outside and lay his body down on the grass the way he used to like—curled sideways, legs tucked up, crooked arms making a pillow for his head. Each day, after they finished exercising his legs, Taylor and Mike would set David up on his side so he could watch them play. Across the street, out behind Lucky's, the other kids would race his wheelchair against the shopping carts.

The best times were in the summer, when they could get David into the city pool. He loved the water and had gotten so he could use his arms pretty good, flapping them around like the busted-up crow Mike let Taylor feed worms to. David was so skinny that

Taylor could wrap her fingers up around his chest, lacing each one in between a rib. She'd hold him up against her chest while Mike worked his legs under water, hollering out, "Yeah, King David! Kick it harder! Ha! I think the little fucker just tried to kick me in the balls!" David would laugh, his head rolling back against Taylor's shoulder, bumping her cheek. After his swimming lesson, Taylor would lay David out curled sideways on a towel so he could watch her and Mike practice backflips and cannonballs off the high dive.

Before David got hit by the car, he was just a snotty-nosed little kid named Davey who got in everyone's way. After he became crippled, though, they started calling him David, sometimes even King David because of how he looked with the fancy red pillow headrest Taylor and Mike had made for his wheelchair. Taylor remembered the day she and Mike stole the pillow from Sears. It was the day she almost flew and Mike got sucker-punched by a biker.

"Tilt him back so he can watch too, okay?" Taylor had hollered down as she prepared to fling her ten-year-old body off the top of the tallest tree in North Hollywood Park.

Mike leaned David's chair against a small pine, bracing the wheels with a couple of rocks. David's scarred and shaven head rolled over to one side.

"No, man, you gotta look up," Mike told him. "Taylor's gonna jump. See her? She's way the fuck up there." Mike made a cushion out of his jacket and propped David's head up, carefully wiping away the thin trail of spit gathering on his brother's chin before he ran back over to spot Taylor's jump.

The first time she fell out of the fifty-foot pine had been an accident; the second time—a jump—was a sucker's dare she couldn't resist. This time it was strictly business. They had made a bet with a couple of bikers, putting down five dollars each that said the barefoot girl with the wild hair and crazy eyes wouldn't jump out of that tree.

Mike and Taylor already had the money spent. They were going to buy David a pillow and make a headrest for his wheelchair.

Crouched down on the strongest branch she could find that high up, Taylor was ready. "Okay, David. This one's for you!" she hollered. She took a deep breath and leapt straight out. It was a perfect jump, far enough out so when she fell she hit the boughs of the branches rather than the unyielding limbs nearer the trunk. For a few blessed moments time stopped. Taylor didn't have to do or think a thing, just relax as gravity sucked her down and the branches bounced her up, breaking her fall and giving her a small taste of freedom. Eyes closed, she smiled to herself and soared. The boys below watched in awe as a skinny body in a torn striped shirt and blue jeans plummeted down, spinning, slamming into branch after branch. Mike, who had seen it all before, began to worry that she was going too fast and sliding out too far on the branches. Nervous, he made the call.

"Taylor!" he yelled. "Taylor, grab on!" She heard his call from far away, waking as if from a dream. Slowly, she reached out to break her fall. The branches that moments ago had softly caressed her now tore through her grasp, slapping against her face. Sensing she was close to hitting the ground, she grabbed on with hands, arms, legs, feet, and toes, curling around the next branch with her entire body, even tucking her chin into her shoulder hoping to catch hold of something. Clinging fiercely to the final branch, she held on tight, bouncing up and down, head spinning, waiting to regain focus. She opened her eyes. Looking back over her shoulder she saw Mike ten feet below, shaking his head.

"Dammit, Taylor," he scowled. "Why you gotta wait till the last fucking branch? I thought I was gonna have to catch you."

"Well, catch me now, okay?" Taylor swung her legs around and dropped down. Mike caught her around the ribs, letting go when he felt her feet touch ground. Dizzy, she fell over. David laughed, "Aaaaah ah aaaaahh."

Mike reached down and picked up the money. "I told you she'd do it, didn't I?"

The older biker slapped Mike up the side of his head, then grabbed him in a half nelson. "Fuck you, punk. You think I'm gonna pay money to watch some crazy bitch jump outta a tree? I think you need to be paying us $10, that's what I think." Tightening his grip on Mike's neck, he lifted him up in the air. "Hey, Jimmy. Take the money."

"Aw man, let him down. The bitch did what he said she'd do. Let's get outta here." Jimmy turned toward his motorcycle. Mike kicked backward, trying to throw an elbow at the same time. The biker yanked Mike's head to the right, bringing his left fist hard into Mike's ribcage.

Taylor ran over and jumped like a monkey onto the guy's back. "Let him go, you stupid motherfucker," she cried, grabbing his hair and reaching for his eyes.

The biker dropped Mike, threw Taylor to the ground like she was a tick he'd picked off his neck, and pulled his knife. "Don't even think of messing with me, you fucking punks, or I'll slit your scrawny throats."

Mike and Taylor froze, crouched on the ground. They could probably outrun the guy by themselves, but they'd never get David out of there. Taylor watched the red-faced biker out of the corner of her eye, remembering how the guy on *Wild Kingdom* said never to look a wild animal straight in the eyes because it will take it as an act of aggression.

"Oh, big man. Taking out a couple of ten-year-olds. What a stud." Jimmy laughed. "Come on, joker, let's go."

"I'm eleven," Mike muttered, rubbing his neck as the two guys rode off with the money, revving their engines.

"Damn, and that was my best jump ever." Taylor stood up and took inventory. "Yeah, that ol' mama tree cut me up a little this time. She don't like it when us mere human beans think we can fly."

"It's *be-ings*," Mike said. "Human beings." She knew he hated the way she talked about the tree like it was a person. Sometimes, when things were rough at home, Taylor would sleep out in the huge old pine, tucking into the tree's thick lower limbs like they were some kind of cradle, oblivious to the beer cans, rubbers, KFC boxes, and partying bikers in the park below.

Mike went to get David. The jacket had slipped loose and David's head was lolling to the side again. Mike kicked one of the rocks. "Goddammit, you think they'd at least get him a wheelchair with a fucking headrest."

Mike had been the oldest in the group of kids walking to school the day his little brother got hit by the car. When David came home from the hospital, senseless and scarred, Mike quietly gathered him alongside his other crippled charges—broken-winged birds, tortoises with cracked shells, cats with busted legs from cars and kicks—and solemnly set to fixing him back up so he could walk again.

"Come on, let's work his legs some before we take him back," Taylor said. They had been working with David almost every day since he'd gotten out of the hospital, exercising his legs like they'd seen on a television show once. The doctor had said the boy might learn to talk again, but he would never walk. Taylor and Mike didn't really care if David talked or not. They understood what his eyes said and knew how to read all his sounds, from the backward laughing "ah ah aaahh"s to the high-pitched train noises he made when he was worried—"wooo ooooh oooh." They also had come to know the complete silences of his terror. Talking didn't matter so much, they thought, but if you were a kid you definitely needed to know how to run.

"Nah, I got something else I want to do," Mike replied. Taylor picked at a scab on her elbow, waiting for Mike to continue. Something was up. He *always* wanted to work on David's legs, no matter what. Mike started walking back home, pushing David along with his right arm. She could tell that biker had really hurt his ribs, but he would never say anything.

"What you gonna do?" Taylor finally asked.

"I'm gonna get him a pillow like I said I was." Mike kicked a small rock out into the street.

Oh, man, thought Taylor. *This is gonna be trouble.* "You know you're gonna need my help," she said. Mike was really smart and her all-time best friend but he couldn't steal worth shit.

Mike kept walking. "I can do it on my own," he muttered.

"Yeah, you can get caught on your own. That's what you can do on your own," Taylor said. "Dang, Mike. You can't hardly even steal a candy bar from Joe's." Joe's was the liquor store where both of their moms sent them each week with signed notes authorizing them to buy cigarettes and whiskey. It was the easiest thing in the world to pocket a Snickers when the clerk turned around to reach for the Pall Mall unfiltereds, but somehow Mike had managed to get caught. Too old for his mom to hit, Mike missed school for a week after his dad got hold of him that night. Bringing up Joe's was a low blow, but Taylor needed to make her point.

"Besides," she continued, "why you so mad at me anyway? It's not my fault that asshole stole our money."

"I'm not mad at you," Mike said. "I'm just mad, that's all."

"Forget it." Taylor reached over and started pushing the left side of the wheelchair. "Come on, let's just get David a pillow. You got a plan?"

"Nah, not really," Mike said. "But I did see a really cool pillow over at Sears."

Taylor looked over at him, raising an eyebrow. "Sears?"

"Yeah, upstairs in the furniture section," he said. "It was on a couch. The sign said, 'Cushions of Crimson Velvet.'"

"Christ," Taylor laughed. "Okay, let me think."

Mike smiled, beginning to relax. Everybody knew Taylor could steal anything that wasn't chained down. They turned the corner by

Taylor's house so she could get cleaned up, stopping short at the sight of the battered old '61 Chevy parked sideways across the lawn. "Uh oh," Mike said. "Your mom's home. We'd better not go in."

Taylor looked at her mom's car, searching for clues. She thought she saw a new dent in the right front fender. She squinted up at the smoggy sky and figured it was close to noon.

"It's okay," Taylor said. "She's probably resting. I'll go in the side window. Wait here, I'll be right back."

"*Resting*," Mike grumbled as Taylor scrambled up the peeling stucco into her bedroom window. "Yeah, right." He reached through the Chevy's open window and took out the bottle of Jack Daniel's lying on the front seat. Pouring out the little that was left, he started to throw the bottle against the back alley wall, but instead quietly stashed it in the bottom of the Jablonskis' trashcan and walked back to wait for Taylor.

A few minutes later she came out, all cleaned up, hair combed, wearing a long-sleeved pink shirt and carrying her grandma's shawl. "Let's go," she smiled. She spread the burgundy shawl over David's lap. "Perfect!"

Sears was just a few blocks away in the Valley Hills Shopping Center. Taylor and Mike took David upstairs to the furniture section on the elevator. Taylor looked around for clerks and plainclothes detectives. *Guess they don't hang out up here in furniture.* The place was empty except for a man and woman looking at dining room tables while their kids jacked the reclining chairs back and forth, spinning each other around.

"Okay, I got it figured," Taylor whispered. "Just hang tight and do what I tell you."

Taylor positioned David's chair right in front the velvet crimson couch and pretended to look at one of the fancy pillows. When she saw a clerk come out to tell the kids to quit playing in the recliner, she whispered to Mike, "Okay, now, pick him up for a minute, okay? Quick."

Mike lifted David up and Taylor jammed the pillow under him, covering up his lap with the shawl. Quickly, she sat back down. Leaning back into the remaining "Cushions of Crimson Velvet," she looked at the price tag and wondered who would ever buy a couch for $300. She smiled at the clerk when he looked their way and then made sure nothing crimson was sticking out from under David's butt.

"Let's go," she whispered.

They took the elevator down and were walking through households toward the exit when Taylor spotted the shiny-shoed detective following them. "I think we'd better buy something," she whispered to Mike. "We look too suspicious."

"We don't *have* any money. Remember?" Mike said, starting to panic. The detective moved in closer, clearly keeping his eyes on them. They would never be able to run with David with them.

"Shit," Taylor said. "Okay, listen. Just look lost and don't say a fucking thing, okay? No matter what." She looked around, trying to appear as helpless as possible, until her eyes settled on the store detective. Then she turned and walked straight up to him.

"Excuse me," she asked. "Do you work here?"

The guy narrowed his eyes. "Why do you ask?"

"My brothers and I, we can't find our mom and we were wondering if you could help us. We were all upstairs and then she went to find a bathroom and now we don't know where she is. We were just gonna go out and see if she was at the car."

"Why don't you come with me instead?" the store detective said. "We'll announce her over the loudspeaker. What is her name?"

Mike looked like he was about to pass out. David rocked a little, softly making his train sound: "Woooo ooooooh wooo." The detective led them over to the waiting room next to gift-wrapping and kitchen utensils.

"Um, Elizabeth," she said, avoiding Mike's stare. "Elizabeth Helen McElroy."

The guy looked hard at her for a moment. "Okay, sit here. I'll call her name up on the PA system." He walked over to a yellow phone on the wall, keeping his eyes on the kids.

"Fuck. What are we gonna do now?" Mike whispered. "We're dead meat."

"No we're not," Taylor said. "He doesn't think we have anything or else he would have taken us into that room over there. It's cool."

"Taylor!" Mike hissed. "It's *not* cool. He's calling our *mom* on the loudspeaker. We don't *have* a mom, remember?" The announcement came through loud: "Mrs. McElroy, please come to customer service. Mrs. McElroy, your children are waiting for you in customer service." The guy leaned back against the wall and lit a cigarette.

"Stay cool," Taylor told Mike. "We just gotta find us a lady, that's all." She quickly scanned the women around her, ruling out the ones that looked too fancy and the ones that looked too poor. She spotted a slow, matronly one fingering the Pyrex. The woman looked like she could make a mean potato salad, change a diaper, and give a good whupping without missing a beat. *Perfect!* Taylor jumped up. "There she is!" she shouted. "Hey, Mom!"

Grinning, she waved at the detective and ran over to the lady with the mixing bowls. "Hey, ma'am, please lady, can you help us? We're here all by ourselves and there's a strange man that's been following us all over the store. My brothers are really scared. I think he might be a molester or something. Could you maybe just pretend to be our mom until he goes away? Please? Please, lady?" She took the startled woman's hand and pointed over to where Mike and David were sitting. Mike definitely looked scared and the man was definitely watching him.

Before the lady could answer, Taylor waved happily over to the boys. Keeping the lady's hand gripped tightly in hers, Taylor hollered out, "Hey, Mike, David, I found her. Come on, let's go!" Mike slowly got up, carefully wheeling David away from the frowning man. Taylor gave him a wave as well and then turned back to the lady. "Those are nice bowls. Can I hold them for you? My mama has bowls just like these. Are you gonna buy them? Is that bad man gone yet? Thank you so much for helping us. I don't know what we would have done without you. You really gotta be careful these days, don't ya?"

At the funeral home, Taylor watched Mike lean over the casket and say goodbye to David. Mike looked old, hard and tired, but it had only been a couple of years since that day they'd stolen the fancy red pillow from Sears and built David a headrest for his wheelchair, strapped together with duct tape and a couple of one-by-twos they'd busted up from a KEEP OUT sign Taylor grabbed on their way home.

Taylor watched Mike's hands tighten on the edge of the casket, his knuckles white. A slight tremor snaked up his arms and back. She could see he was fighting to keep his jaw clenched but the tremor transformed into a shake. Taylor watched in horror as Mike's whole body convulsed. At first there was no sound except for the soft pounding of Mike's head on the edge of the coffin. Then his body became racked with sobs, long rough moans that sounded more like they came from a tortured animal than a thirteen-year-old boy.

Taylor had never seen Mike cry. He said he never had. Not when he broke his arm playing street football. Not when he fell from his garage roof onto the unfinished concrete wall in the back alley, landing on a piece of rusted rebar. Not even when his dad took the belt to him after they got home from the hospital, tearing up the unbandaged flesh of his skinny, shirtless back.

"Never cry" was the number one rule governing survival if you were born into the Doyle family. It was a rule they had tried to teach the middle boy, Ryan, ever since they could remember—lesson after lesson after lesson, usually huddled in the back closet after a beating. But Ryan, Ryan was a crier. That boy never learned how *not* to cry. His mom would just look at him sideways and he'd start bawling, and once he got started Mike was the only one who could calm him down. But now Mike was the one sobbing, ragged howls, feral, unleashed. Taylor felt like she was going to be sick. The room began to spin and she left her body to watch from the top of the chapel. She saw Ryan panic, get up, and run red-faced out into the street, and she remembered the morning two weeks ago when everything began to break apart.

It was that hot, sticky summer dawn when she'd heard something hit up against her bedroom window.

"Taylor, get up! You gotta come help me," Mike was whisper-shouting from the walkway below. Her room was at the end of the house, just across from the Doyles' living room. She heard everything that went on in the Doyle house and could tell from the sounds which kid was getting beaten or whipped. Mike was too big for his mom to hit. Tommy was trying to get big fast but wasn't quite there yet, so when Mrs. Doyle cupped her hand against the side of his head it sounded like a pumpkin dropped off a roof. Before David's accident, he and Sean made exactly the same quick squeal of outrage and then became real quiet because they knew it only made their mom madder when they cried. Pretty soon she'd stop and they'd go running back outside to play.

Ryan was the problem because no matter what they tried, he couldn't stop crying when his mom yelled at him. Taylor had spent the morning listening to the high-pitched wail: "RY-AN, WHY ARE YOU CRY-ING?" Whup! "RY-AN, STOP YOUR CRY-ING!" Whup! Every time Mrs. Doyle yelled, Ryan cried. Every time he cried, she belted him again and he cried harder. Taylor had heard it a hundred times before. She knew there was nothing to be done until she heard the silence that meant Ryan had been knocked unconscious, or the loud music that meant Mrs. Doyle had given up and was trying to drown him out. Either way, Taylor knew she'd find Ryan locked in the back closet on the other side of the house.

It was the silence Taylor had been listening to when she heard Mike at her window. They had the routine down by now, but it hadn't always been that way. The first time Taylor tried to help Ryan, she learned her body could make the same thick sound hitting against the wall as any boy bodies Mrs. Doyle flung that way. It had happened when she and Mike climbed in through the back window and unlocked the closet to get to Ryan. He was bleeding from a cut above his eye and softly moaning, too dazed to even cry. Taylor stood back a little, watching Mike cradle his brother on the floor of the closet. She was trying to figure out where she was going to get Ryan a jar to pee in, which was the only thing he wanted, when Mrs. Doyle came bursting into the room. Taylor couldn't get out of the way. She felt her right arm jerked out of its socket, her left side slam into the wall, and in between she flew.

Taylor slid down the wall to the floor, trying to find air. Mike ran out of the room, getting backhanded across the head. Unable to move, Taylor crouched in terror as Mrs. Doyle picked up the bloody child and began rocking him back and forth.

"Ry Ry, what's wrong, baby? Mommy's here. You know you're my baby. You know Mommy loves you best."

That was the thing about Ryan. You couldn't ever tell if he was going to get hit or held. When Taylor could get her breath, she ran.

After that, Mike and Taylor perfected their rescue techniques. They decided Taylor would go to the front door and cause a distraction while Mike and Tommy snuck in through the back window with warm washcloths, water, and a pee jar. Since Taylor didn't belong to Mrs. Doyle, she was the least likely to get hit in the moments following an explosion. Plus, she was the closest thing to a girl in the neighborhood, even if she could kick the butt of every boy around. Her mom once told her that part of what made Mrs. Doyle nuts was, one, that she was married to Mr. Doyle and, two, that she kept trying and trying for a girl baby, but they kept coming out boys—Mike, Tom, Ryan, Dave, Sean, Bobby—till finally she snapped and went crazy, probably around Ryan. All Taylor knew was she was scared shitless of this woman built like a halfback, who could throw her across the room like a little piece of nothing.

But on that one hot, sticky summer morning when it all began to break apart, it was precisely because she was peacefully listening to the silence that Taylor was so surprised to hear Mike knocking at her bedroom window. She went over to the window, climbed up on the dresser, and looked down at her friend.

"Hurry up, Taylor," Mike whispered. "I think Ryan's hurt bad."

Taylor climbed out the window, thinking hard. She looked to the street. Mr. Doyle's car was gone. It was too early in the morning to borrow David. He wouldn't be dressed yet. Mrs. Doyle didn't like to loan cigarettes, bacon was too expensive, and Taylor had already borrowed sugar twice that week. Maybe a little margarine, she thought. That might work. Plus she could make it a really girl thing and ask Mrs. Doyle about a recipe for something. Last time she'd helped Mrs. Doyle do the grocery shopping she discovered the ten ways to use Hamburger Helper so your family doesn't know they're eating the same thing every night.

"Okay, I got it," Taylor said. "Do you need any towels?"

"Nah, I got some," Mike said. "Try and give me at least ten minutes, okay?" Mike took off around the back side of the house before she could answer.

"Yeah. I'll try," Taylor replied, slowly walking up to the Doyle's front porch. She took a deep breath and knocked on the front door. There was no answer. She waited another minute and then knocked again, harder. Still nothing. She grew worried that Mrs. Doyle might be heading toward the back room where Ryan was. She thought of running around the house and warning Mike, but she didn't want to *not* be there if Mrs. Doyle answered the door. Closing her eyes and leaning her head on the doorway, Taylor wished she were somewhere else. Anywhere else. She felt her stomach rise and her heart sink. She knocked really hard a third time and then tried the door. It opened and she entered the living room, hollering out as loud as she could, "Hey, Mrs. Doyle, are you home? It's me, Taylor. Can I talk to you?"

The navy blue sheets Mrs. Doyle used for curtains were all drawn shut and the room smelled of stale Pall Malls and Wild Turkey. Taylor felt her stomach lurch at the familiar odor. The front door had closed behind her and she could hardly see without the morning light. She took a few steps toward the kitchen. "Mrs. Doyle," she called. "Are you home?" She heard a bump in the back bedroom where Ryan was locked up in the closet. Then something moved right beside her and she jumped at the sight of Mrs. Doyle sitting silent in the center of the room.

Inside she screamed and ran, but out loud she stayed and said, "Oh, Mrs. Doyle, you scared me. I'm sorry to bother you. I didn't know you were sleeping. My mom asked if I could come over and maybe borrow some margarine. We're getting ready to make some French toast. You ever made French toast? My mom said you might know how."

Mrs. Doyle glared past her, stood up, and slowly made her way into the kitchen, steadying herself on the back of the old grey sofa. Taylor followed behind, smelling before she actually saw them the crusty dishes and pans, the open, half-empty cans of Chef Boy-Ar-Dee and SpagettiOs littering the table and countertops. Over in the corner she saw Sean sitting on the floor with the baby, tearing off crusts of Wonderbread, making up hard little balls with the white insides, placing them carefully in patterns only his eyes could see. Sean rolled the doughy balls back and forth on the floor while Bobby patted around on the pile of discarded crusts. Mrs. Doyle handed Taylor half a stick of margarine. The girl took it, flinching slightly at the touch of Mrs. Doyle's clammy hand, feeling how soft and warm the margarine was even though it had just come out of the refrigerator.

Mrs. Doyle glared at her. Taylor knew she was supposed to leave, but it hadn't been ten minutes yet. "So, do you know how to make this stuff?" Taylor asked. "I think you put the bread in eggs and then fry it up, but I'm not sure. Have you ever made French toast?"

Mrs. Doyle walked slowly past Taylor into the living room. Taylor had never seen her like this, hollow and mute, like something out of the *Night of the Living Dead*. The girl knew she had to do something to keep Mrs. Doyle from walking back down the hall to the closet room. Rushing around in front of her, Taylor blocked the hallway, stopping in front of the room she knew David slept in.

"Is David up yet?" Taylor asked. "Can I take him out for a walk today?" She looked into the room, swallowing the bile that rose in her throat. David was lying on a pile of old sheets, having attempted to crawl away from the corner where he had shit. Taylor grabbed his wheelchair, making as much noise as possible. "Can I help you get him dressed?" she asked.

Mrs. Doyle sat down on the edge of the bunk bed Ryan and Sean slept on. Hunched over, she stared at her hands, as if she were trying to remember something. Taylor grabbed some dirty clothes off the floor and started dressing David, wiping the rest of his shit off onto the sheets. By the time she got him into his chair and out the door, she figured it had to have been enough time for Mike to tend to Ryan.

Taylor wheeled David down to the park, where she knew Mike would come looking for her. Settling, Taylor leaned up against the base of her favorite tree, pressing her cheek into the warm, rough bark. She chewed on a handful of long grass she had picked up on the way. By the time Mike found her, she was holding onto the thick tree, puking.

Mike put his hand on her shoulder. "Come on, let's work his legs some, okay?"

Late that night Taylor woke to the methodical sound of pumpkin blows and silent cries. She knew by the sound of creaking metal that

it was David being hit. She thought of his crimson red headrest. She
thought of the train sounds he made in the Sears' customer service
area. *Woooo woooooo wooooo.* She thought of the way her fingers fit
so perfectly in between his ribs at the city pool as he flapped and
splashed around. She thought and thought of something she could
go borrow. She looked at the alarm clock by the side of the bed. It
was three in the morning. Each metallic blow rocked through her
slight frame, pinning her down. She tried to swing her legs over and
get up out of bed, but they felt like cement blocks. She could only
move her arms; her eyes thrashed wildly in her head. She felt a huge
boulder crushing into her chest, letting in only the thinnest stream
of air. "*Oooooo. Ooooooo.*"

She lay there for a long time until the pumpkin sounds stopped
and the dawn broke. Then she lay there some more. Around ten the
next morning she heard the wailing cry of a siren rush up next door.
Standing on shaky legs, Taylor looked out her bedroom window.
Mr. Doyle's car was still not there. She saw three medics run into
the Doyles' house and then emerge slowly, wheeling something on a
cart. She heard muffled voices. Sliding down out her window, Taylor
crouched in the bushes, watching the small gathering of neighbors
in front of David's house.

"What happened?" asked one.

"That crippled kid fell out of his chair and hit his head," answered
another.

"Just a damn shame."

Hair wrapped up tight in lime green curlers, Mrs. Jablonski set
her coffee cup down on the sidewalk, pulling rosary beads out of the
pocket of her orange floral robe. "Yes," she said. "A shame but also a
blessing. God has finally brought deliverance to that poor sick boy
trapped inside that simple brain and useless body."

Behind them, Taylor saw Mike fly down the street, riding hard,
the old black shoebox where he kept the wounded crow strapped
tight to the handlebars of his bicycle.

when i was a little girl

when i was a little girl i had a favorite tree. i'd run across the city streets to the park where she grew tall, and with determined fingers and stubby little toes, i'd find familiar holds and climb up to the top. spiraling up her lovely roughened trunk, limbs reaching out for limbs (i knew she reached for me, too), i'd press my cheek warm into her bark, tuck my sleepy body into her waiting arms, and sometimes i would doze. safe and held by strong pine branches, cradled, rocked by western winds, what could be wrong with a picture such as this?

what's wrong with this picture is that it is three o'clock in the morning, the santa ana winds are blowing, and the child is all alone fifty feet in the air. what's wrong is that it is three o'clock in the l.a. morning, the child is five, six, seven, eight years old and so afraid she does not even feel her fear. besides, she cannot cry, because just below in the soiled city park, the chain boys gather to fight and fuck whatever comes their way.

what's wrong with this picture is that this is one of the lucky nights, when the child has won sleep's slow-motion race and beat the footsteps coming down the hall, tumbling out her bedroom window into the *streets below. what's wrong is that it is three o'clock in the morning, the child is all alone fifty feet in the air, so afraid she does not even know it, and this is one of the lucky nights when she does not have to look down from the corner of the yellowed ceiling and watch what happens to that strangely damp and quiet girl lying in her bed below.*

The First Thing You Need to Know

The first thing you need to know as you enter this house is how to get out. The easiest way is to just not come in at all, but sometimes you will have to, especially at dusk or when you hear your first *and* middle name hollered out from the front porch. Once inside the house, if you're lucky, you can just take a quick left turn through the kitchen and head out the back door, careful to not let the screen door slam. There, you will be greeted by a wiggling muscle-bound Boxer mix named Bucky who will always be happy to see you.

This will prove to be a very important thing, so make sure you become good friends with Bucky. And, soon you won't even care that his long slips of gooey slobber sometimes shake loose and land on you when you pet him, because the thing about Bucky is that he will let you come inside his doghouse whenever you want. His body is soft and always warm and you can just come curl up with him if you need a place to hide or maybe to just take a little rest.

If you don't take the kitchen door exit, things become a bit trickier. You will go down the long hallway, past your mom and grandma's rooms on the right and the bathroom on your left. None of these rooms will have a way out. At the end of the hall is your room and you will feel lucky to not have to share with your grandma anymore, but you will also be afraid. The best thing about your room is that there is a big aluminum sliding-glass window that opens out onto the alley between your house and the next door neighbor's. This window will become your most common way in and out of the house.

At night, from your bed you will listen for your mom's car because you know it is your job to bring her home safe. You will picture her leaving the bar, laughing and arguing with her union friends, stumbling to the battered Chevy Impala, dumping her purse upside down in the El Chorito parking lot to find her keys. You will picture her getting on the Hollywood Freeway, bearing left onto the 101. "Don't speed Mama," you will tell her. "Stay in between the lines." You will help her remember to signal for the exit, to slow down for the off ramp and come to a complete stop at the corner of Lankershim and Laurel Canyon where the cops like to hang out. At this point, you will relax a little because you know if she hits something she'll be going pretty slow and she can probably just back it up and continue on towards home. When she pulls into the driveway, you will listen especially carefully. If she turns in sharp and brakes fast, you might as well just pack it up and head out the bedroom window right then and there, because you know it will be you who pays for whatever has pissed her off. But if she pulls in easy, doesn't spin the gravel, and maybe just slow bumps the trash cans, you're probably gonna be okay.

Quickly, you will run through the list in your head. Did you clean up the kitchen good, put away the dishes, leave her a plate in the fridge in case she's hungry? Did you clear away any junk that might be in the path from the front door to her bedroom? Is the Folgers measured just right in the tall silver coffee pot so all she has to do is turn it on when she wakes up and her morning coffee will be just the way she likes it? Is the dog locked out back? Did you leave the front door unlocked for your mom so she doesn't have to mess with her keys? Is your grandma tucked in bed and did you remember to take her teeth out and clean them before you put them in the jar on her bed stand? Are the bills where your mom can't see them until she's sobered up? Did you remember to wash her red nightgown and lay it out on her bed?

From your bed you will listen to hear if the front door slams or if it shuts slowly with the weight of her body as she leans back, exhausted. You will listen to hear if she stops at her bedroom or keeps coming down the hall. This will be a tricky moment because the bathroom is right before your bedroom, and if she needs help, you will need to be there. So, you will listen for the footsteps coming down the hall and if they are shuffling and you hear her bump the walls, then you will know she is headed for the bathroom, probably to puke. If so, you will need to get in there fast, pull her long black hair up for her, wet a clean cloth with warm water and wipe her brow, clean the strings of vomit from her hair, her face, her shirt. Or, if it's a hot, dry night and the Santa Ana winds are blowing, you know she wants the cloth wet with really cool water laid across the back of her neck. Then, when she is done puking, you will clean her up, help her brush her teeth, help her make it down the hall, into her nightgown and put to bed. Then, just before she passes out, she will say, "Oh honey. You are an absolute angel. I don't know what I would do without you," and you will think you should be proud and happy, and maybe just a little bit you are, but when you go back down the hall to finish cleaning up the bathroom, you will not know why you also feel like you kind of want to cry.

Some nights from your bed you will listen for her footsteps and if they come heavy and lurching down the hall, then you will need to make it to the window fast. When this happens, even if she tries to grab you on your way out, *do not stop*. Kick her if you must because she probably will not remember anyway and whatever whupping you may get the next day will be nothing compared to what will happen if you stay. Under no circumstances should you let yourself get trapped inside the bathroom with her when she is in her angry drunk. If you make a mistake and try to help her on nights like this, make sure your body is positioned between her and the door so you can take off if she turns. Do not, I repeat, do not ever let her get between you and the bathroom door, even on the good nights. Tender skulls, usually yours, are no match for the porcelain sink, toilet bowl and bathtub ledge and once the floors get slippery with blood, you will have less traction than a wet dog in a soapy bathtub. Grabbing onto the shower curtain will not help.

So, if you can, the best bet is to just climb out the bedroom window right from the jump. There, you will drop down into the alley, careful not to get scraped up on the rough stucco wall. From there you will have two choices. If the bikers are already partying in the park across the street, you will circle around through the alley and hop the fence into your own backyard and see if Bucky will scoot over and let you sleep with him for a while. But if the park is clear, your best shot is to climb up your favorite tree and just settle in for the night. Once you climb up past the first set of lower limbs, you will notice two thick branches which grow straight out, side by side, with only a little gap between them, making a perfect cradle for your butt and legs. Then, you can just lean back against the strong trunk and not have to worry about anything until it starts to get light.

There will be some nights when from your bed you will hear your mom's car pull up nice and easy into the driveway. You will hear her key in the door, even though you left it unlocked. When she comes in the house, you will hear her whistle for the dog. "Hey Bucky," she will call. "Come here pretty boy." You will hear her open the cupboard and pour herself a shot of bourbon. You will hear the ice clink lightly in the glass. If you are really lucky, you will hear her softly singing. If it's Frank Sinatra's "Fly Me to the Moon," you will know she is happy and it's going to be a good night. Even though she cannot carry a tune, you will love it when she sings, "I dreamed I saw Joe Hill last night, alive as live can be…" and your favorite, "Oh you can't scare me, I'm stickin' to the Union."

You will know she's had a good day and that you can probably talk her into telling you old union stories when she comes into your room to say goodnight. "Ha!" she will laugh, sitting down on your bed. You will scooch over to make room for her. She will take a drink and say, "Oh, honey, you should have seen Gwen and I take on the management boys of Del Monte Canning Company today. There we were," she will say, taking a long drag off her Marlboro, "sitting at the arbitration table with all the heavy hitters lined up, ten of them and just the two of us, those goons in suits all throwing their power around like the little pompous pricks they are. Well," she will continue, "one of them went just a little too far tonight and damned if Gwen didn't just calmly reach over onto the center of the table, grab one of those bowls of fancy canned peaches they had set out for us, and dump it, sticky syrup and all, right into that joker's lap!"

Your mom will throw her head back and laugh and you will take that opportunity to slide in just a little closer so it will almost feel like she is holding you. If you are really lucky, she will tell stories about when she marched through Delano, arm in arm with Dolores Huerta and Cesar Chavez, or better yet, stories of you as a baby. "They told me not to take you out of the house for the first few weeks," she will say. "But I just told them, 'Screw that! I've got work to do.' So I just bundled you up, put you in your little stroller, and off we went, marching up and down that picket line on Wilshire, wind blowing in our faces, carrying signs and singing at the top of our lungs." And you will close your eyes and almost be able to remember what it felt like to be tucked into that little stroller, bundled all safe and warm, pushed up and down the picket line with your mom and her great union friends. These will be the nights when your heart nearly bursts with pride and excitement and when you want to *never* fall asleep. But these will be the nights when you do, finally, sleep.

sometimes on sundays

sometimes on sundays, she would put her teeth in and we would go to church. singing light and praying fierce, she'd cut daytime deals with the father she so loved and feared. bargains neither one of them would ever keep.

sometimes on sundays, i'd cram wild toes in pinchy shoes and we would go to church. holding my small hand in hers, she'd press old coins into my palms, and i'd grumble every time i placed them on that shiny plate for god.

sometimes on sundays, i'd grow furious with this god who'd take these coins from children and then forsake them in the night. this god who sacrificed his only son. this god who never even tried to answer my grandma's wet and toothless cries, as i stood helpless by her bed, holding her hand, stroking her arm, trembling into dawn.

Lemon Zest

"Okay, honey, now give it some zest!" Taylor's grandma laughed, eyes sparkling, and Taylor's heart lifted at the signal to start grating tiny slivers of lemon peel into the large yellow bowl. Standing beside her grandmother at the sink, making lemon meringue pies, Taylor was careful to not let her knuckles get scraped on the grater, though sometimes it did happen. She made sure her grandmother didn't see because then she might not trust the young girl with the best part of this venture: the moment she handed Taylor the big knife and let her cut the lemons in half for squeezing.

Ever since her grandmother had moved in, Taylor had watched in awe as this strange, tall, gruff, God-fearing woman cut everything from bread to onions, carrots, potatoes and ham. She had carried the old, heavy-handled nine-inch blade with her through the Depression, the challenge of a fickle God and a cheating husband, and it was the only knife she'd cook with. Stained dark with time and use, the wood handle had a slight burn and four small circular rust marks where the blade attached. For years Taylor's mom tried to get her to throw that knife away, but her grandmother just scoffed at the fancy new stainless steel blades. "They just don't cut right," she would say. "Heck, I don't care about a little bit of rust. I just need a knife that can cut."

After her first stroke was when Taylor's grandmother began to let the girl hold the knife, and help her with that part of the cooking. "It's all up to you now, honey," she'd said. "I just can't do nothing with this right paw anymore."

Taylor finished grating the peel and looked up at her grandmother for permission to cut the lemons, the only part of this Saturday morning pie-making operation that required a knife. Her grandmother gave a slight nod and Taylor opened the drawer and pulled out the heavy blade. Standing tall at the sink, careful to show her grandmother that she remembered how to hold her fingers just so, away from the blade, Taylor reached for the lemons and was just beginning to cut when her mother stormed through the kitchen, purse and car keys in hand, late for work.

"What the hell do you think you're doing?" her mom yelled, spotting Taylor at the cutting board. "You know I told you not to touch that damn knife. Put that thing down right this minute. Mother, what did I tell you about letting that girl handle a knife? She's too young. It's just too damn dangerous for a child." She looked at her watch. "Damn," she said. "And now you've gone and made me late." Shaking her head in disgust, Taylor's mom walked out, letting the back door slam behind her.

Taylor froze, slowly placing the knife down on the counter. Heart racing, she held perfectly still and listened. Once she heard the engine crank and the car pull out the drive, she relaxed a bit and began to breathe. Still, she didn't move.

Still humming and rolling out the dough with her one good hand, Taylor's grandmother looked down at the frozen girl. "Honey, what's wrong?" she asked.

Taylor stood still, one hand down by her side, the other resting inches from the blade.

Her grandmother wiped the flour from her good left hand onto her apron and put her arm around Taylor's shoulder. "Ah, honey," she said, pulling the girl close. "Is it your mom? Don't mind her. She knows better than that foolishness. Saying a child like you can't handle a simple knife." She sucked her teeth, making a tsking sound. "Besides, I'm the one who taught her, just like my daddy taught me. He'd say, 'Child, just handle it. Whatever it is. Handle your business. Handle your fear. Because whatever you can't handle is just going to come back round and handle you.' That's how I was raised and that's how I raised your mama."

She reached down and picked up the knife, carefully handed it to Taylor. "Here, child," she said. "Take this. You're just fine. Go ahead now, cut."

Taylor took the knife in her left hand and with her right picked up the first lemon, holding it steady, firm grip, knuckles out, keeping the blade away from her fingertips just like her grandmother had shown her. Taking a breath, with one smooth slice she cut through the lemon, smiling as the left half fell away, glistening, on the cutting board.

"That's right, honey. You're just fine." Taylor's grandmother wiped her hand and picked up the rolling pin, turning back to her dough, softly singing now instead of humming, "Nearer, my God, to thee, nearer to thee…"

Taylor reached for the pile of lemons and sliced through one after another, each with one smooth, simple stroke, the knife perfectly balanced in her small hand, the juice slightly stinging in the scrapes on her knuckles.

a quick snapping of the trap

i am not the soft brown mouse ambling down the trail, coming upon the yellow cheese propped here and there to find, nibbling along her way. picked up! suddenly rising in the air, thick thumb and fingers circling her belly. her tiny feet scrambling. her tiny heart exploding. put down to face another way. here's some water. here's some cheese. here's another wall. and i am not the sleek grey rat who races, stands and sniffs, turning corners with ferocious speed, precision cuts that do not touch the walls. the darting mind that fully knows its maze, yet still thinks there is a way. no longer bothering to stop and eat the hardened cakey cheese. and i am not the white and dying one, pink eyed, missing tufts of hair, though she knows who it is i am, and we watch together as the walls come closer. hands reach in, replacing wooden slats with shiny mirrors, some streaked with blood and shit. whose? hands which mostly leave, but sometimes come to push, to prod, as the big red faces peer down and wonder why she no longer tries to find her way. what went wrong with the experiment? how once she ran so quick. how once she cringed when the hands reached in—four legs peddling the hot thin air, wild heart beating, body stiff. how once she turned to bite. but who really wants to taste such flesh? i tell you these things so you know how i feel about *outstretched hands, so you know i can't be picked up and taken from the maze. for i am not the soft brown mouse, and i am not the sleek grey rat, and i am not the white and dying one. i am what got left when recognition shattered. so don't mistake this hen's headless twitching for some thing you know as life. the bodies die, the walls cave in. there is no way. i am just a point of pain, a quick snapping of the trap.*

A Fire that Had to Burn

Taylor woke from a furious sleep to the sound of her mother's car careening up the drive. She knew how to read all the sounds that puke-brown Chevy Impala could make and she could tell from the protesting creaks on the last turn by her bedroom that it had been a whiskey kind of night down at the "union hall" everybody else knew as Ernie's Bar, and that she was in for a fight.

Her mom had been organizing workers in bars and pool halls ever since she could remember, and she knew the late nights and drinking were never gonna change. "But baby," her mom would explain, "you know I can't meet with the machinists until they get off their last shift, and if they want a drink, well what can I say? We've almost got that contract wrapped up. We can't stop now. *Someone's* got to look after their rights."

"Yeah, Mom, I know," Taylor would answer, her stock reply.

Right now, however, Taylor had to quick jerk her jeans on and her mind out of its last bit of sleep because she knew this was not going to be a "yeah, Mom, I know" kind of night. She heard the engine die as the old Chevy rammed the plastic trashcans at the back end of the garage and choked to a stop.

When she was young Taylor had been afraid that car would crash right through her bedroom window, burying her in a pile of splintered wood and shattered glass, the metal beast finally coming to rest with its steaming radiator spitting down on her face and chest. But it never did, always making that last turn, although sometimes it took out part of the scrubby bush beside her window. More often than not the car's embattled body encountered some piece or other of the garage's equally beleaguered frame, a frame Taylor was determined to keep standing.

She felt a small rush of satisfaction that the trashcans had done their job. That afternoon she had strategically placed the two cans, filled with dirt and weeds, by the one remaining decent two-by-four holding up the back wall of the garage. Taylor had almost gotten busted stealing sheetrock the month before from the construction site down on 24th Street and, even though two-by-fours were much easier to steal than sheetrock, she knew the contractors would be looking out for her and she'd have to lay low for a while. She had hoped to lift some lumber from the gas station they were building around the corner, but her friend Mario was the only Mexican working on the construction crew and she knew he'd be fired if anything turned up missing.

Taylor heard the front door slam. Too late to make it out the bedroom window, she knew she had made the mistake of lingering too long in her trashcan satisfaction. She heard her mom coming down the hall and knew her room was next.

"Goddammit, girl, how many times do I have to tell you to put shit away? I ran right into those damn trashcans you left lying around and it just about scared me to death." Her mom balanced against the bedroom door, swaying slightly.

"I'm sorry, Mama." Taylor took a step back, wondering if she could still make it to the window. Her bag lay by the closet to her mom's left, just out of reach. She felt tired. A sludgy, familiar mist crept up her back and neck and she knew there was no way out.

"Sorry don't mean shit, young lady! I'll show you sorry." Taylor's mom took an unsteady step forward. Taylor stood still, ready to catch her if she fell, ready to block a blow.

She watched the cigarette smoke curling out of her mother's red-smeared mouth. It worried her that she hadn't seen her mother inhale. She made a quick mental note to pay better attention to the stained left hand holding one of the Pall Mall unfiltereds she bought her mom each week down at Joe's Liquors. It was the reason she missed the right hand coming up against the side of her head.

"Pay attention when I'm talking to you, goddammit," her mother yelled, her voice husky and raw.

Taylor cursed the tears that came with a slap even though she refused to cry out. "I'm sorry, Mama," she said. "Come on—it's late. Let me put you to bed." Taylor reached for her mother's arm.

"You're not putting me anywhere until you do some explaining," her mom said, pulling away. Taylor knew "explaining" was a dead-end trick. No, she wouldn't play that one anymore, though there was little else to play on nights like this. If she cooked dinner and her mom didn't come home, she was careless and wasteful of food. If she didn't make dinner, she was lazy, worthless, and ungrateful. If she didn't clean the house right, she was a no-good freeloader taking advantage of her hardworking mother. If she cleaned it too good, she was trying to shame her mother and pretend to be something better than she was. No, this was not something to be explained. This was just a fire that had to burn.

"Mama, I said I was sorry. It won't happen again. I'll put the cans up right next time, okay? Let's go to bed." Taylor tried to make her voice something louder than a mumble, but still soft, calm—an engaged monotone.

The left hand caught her square across her face and she felt the warmth of blood sliding out her nose. Furious that she hadn't seen that one coming either, the girl raised her arm to block the next unseen blow and accidentally knocked the cigarette out of her mother's hand. They both stared in shock at the little glow burning into the dirty beige carpet. Neither moved. Then, slowly, Taylor bent down for the cigarette, ready to come back up with another "I'm sorry" when she got hit on the side of her head.

What the fuck! Knocked down onto one knee, Taylor moved quickly into a crouch, body coiled. *Stay down,* she told herself. *Just stay down.* She tried to will herself to breathe, calm, take inventory. Her nose was starting to bleed again, and a fresh new cut had opened up by her left eye where her mom's ring must have hit. She felt no pain, just an irritating tickle of blood dripping down her face, small drops turning brown as they hit the floor. *Nothing you can't handle,* she thought, but inside she felt something crack open, a hot burn splintering down her chest and back into her arms. *Stay down,* she warned, but her body sprang forward, slamming her mom against the wall. From far away she thought she heard someone scream, "Don't you dare raise your hand to your mother," but inside she felt a strange quiet and the curious sensation of her hands circling her mother's neck, raising her effortlessly up against the hallway door. She was only fourteen, but she was taller than her mom, whose body felt surprisingly small and light. Taylor saw her own skinny arms pinning her mom to the door, saw her mom's feet kicking at the air in slow futility. She felt no anger, just the fullness of hot lava flowing through her body. The terror would come soon, leaving her trembling on the pavement, sobbing on the cold night streets, but for now, the empty cavern in her chest felt full, warm.

There seemed no real reason for her to release rather than squeeze but that is what she did, and she watched as her mother fell in a heap to the floor. The girl turned and picked up the bag she kept packed with boots, jeans, her three favorite t-shirts, and her Levi jacket. She took the heavy, scuffed boots out of her bag and pulled them on. She looked at the four books sitting in the bag. The clothes stayed the same, but every night Taylor argued amicably with herself about what books to bring. Constant were *Charlotte's Web* and *The Yearling*, her two all-time favorites. She was looking at the two new ones she had just stolen, *Soul on Ice* and a book by Gandhi on nonviolence, when she heard the heap begin to cry.

"Baby, what are you doing? Where you going? You're not going to leave me. You know you're my best thing. You're the only one who understands me. Come here, baby. You know I love you the best. I'm sorry you got such a mess of a mama. Come on, help me to bed, okay?" Her mother reached out her arms, pleading.

Taylor looked over at the crumpled pile. Her mom's legs were folded at an awkward angle; the cigarette continued to burn on the floor. Taylor watched the blackened circle spread on the worn brown carpet for a moment before rubbing it out with her boot. She bent to pick her mother up, then carried her to the bed. Her mom's head rolled against her shoulder and Taylor fought off nausea as her mom's hair touched her cheek. Laying her gently down on the bed, Taylor put a blanket over the trembling form, still amazed at how small her mother seemed. She pulled off her mother's shoes, turned out the lights, picked up the bag with all four books in it, and climbed out the window into the streets below.

PART TWO

Steal Away

Telling Stories

"Whatcha doin'?" Taylor called out, popping her head into the back of the camper. She saw Jackson sitting in her usual spot, writing. "Why don't you put that shit down for a while and come get high with me," she said. "You've had your head buried in that journal all damn day." Pulling out a freshly rolled fatty, she waved it in front of her girlfriend. "I think you're gonna like this." She grinned.

Jackson sat curled up on the floor, the coolest afternoon spot in the camper, her journal balanced between her knees. "I tell you what, girl," she said, leaning back. "I'll give you half of what you want. I'll get high with you and then I'll go back to writing."

"Ah, shit," Taylor groaned. "You're working the best end of that deal. As usual." She climbed inside, put her gear down, and pulled off her boots. "What you writing, anyway?" she asked. "Another letter to your mom?"

"Nah," Jackson said. "Actually, I'm writing a story. Come on." She patted the floor beside her. "Let's fire that nasty thing up."

Taylor lit the joint and gave Jackson the first serious hit. Jackson held it for a moment and then leaned over and kissed her, blowing the smoke deep into her lungs. "Umm," Taylor sighed, exhaling.

"Now isn't this way better than writing?" She passed the joint to Jackson. "What's your story about, anyway?"

Jackson took a long hit, holding it in as long as she could. She exhaled slowly, smiling. "It's about us," she said. "The first time we met."

"Serious?" Taylor said, sitting up. "You're writing a fucking story about us? Can I read it?"

Jackson laughed. "Oh, now all of a sudden girl's interested in my writing," she teased.

"No, I'm serious," Taylor said. "Let me read it."

Jackson took another hit before passing the joint back to Taylor. "Tell you what," she said. "I'll let you read my story on one condition." She laughed as Taylor groaned. "First, you have to write your own damn story and then you can hear mine. Instead of giving me so much shit about my writing, I think you should write something. Then we'll swap. Come on, girl. Just try it."

"I don't know how to write a story," Taylor complained. "You know I never passed a damn English class in my life." She was just starting to get a nice buzz and now things were getting complicated. All she wanted was to get high and hang out for a while, not to have to work for it.

"That shit doesn't matter," Jackson argued. "You read all the fucking time and can't shut up when you start telling your damn stealing stories. Girl, I know you can write."

"What do I write about?" Taylor asked, sullen, giving up.

Jackson pushed her and laughed. "Ah, baby. Don't go getting all attitudinal on me now. Just write about the same thing. Write about how we met. Just tell a story. Hell, I know you can do that."

Taylor grabbed a pen and some paper and climbed up into the overhead sleeping bunk, ignoring the heat, taking the joint with her. She lay down on her back, stretched her legs out the full length of the bed, and sighed. She thought about the first time she had seen Jackson, how the girl had always caught her eye but they'd never talked. She thought about how she'd secretly wished it had been Jackson who'd cut up that trick who'd harassed her, but hadn't known for sure. She thought about the first time they'd actually met, how she'd seen Jackson cornered in an ally without her knife. *Okay*, she thought. *I can tell that story.* She relit the joint and began to write.

A half hour later, she heard Jackson get up and come over to the bunk.

"Okay," Jackson said. "I've been hearing some scribbling going on up there. Plus, you've been seriously bogarting that joint. Come on. Let me see what you've got." She climbed up on the bed and curled against Taylor, reaching for the paper. Snuggling in, her head on Taylor's shoulder, she read:

I jumped before I thought. Came around the corner, seen one brother slug her, the other pull his blade. Seen her head snap back, hit hard against the wall. Seen her knife slide away, outta reach, glistening like a tease under the sticky green dumpster. I seen her knees buckle, high heel boots crumple, pink tube top doubling over a black vinyl miniskirt. I knew right away who it was. Yeah, I been watching that one real close. Tough skinny black girl. Tall, wiry, nothin' extra, nothin' wasted. Just enough.

"Damn, girl," Jackson laughed. "That's a trip. You write just the way you talk."

"What's wrong with that?" Taylor asked. "How am I supposed to write?"

"It's cool, baby," Jackson said. She reached over and put her hand on Taylor's belly. "It's your style. Ain't nothing wrong with that. You just jump right in and get right down to business, that's all. Sometimes writers just get, I don't know, maybe a little more *literary* about it, that's all."

Taylor snatched the piece of paper back. "Literary," she frowned. "What the fuck. Besides, this ain't how I talk." She read through her story, then pointed to a line. "Look at this," she said. "Your knife was 'glistening like a tease under the sticky green dumpster.' Damn," she laughed, putting the paper down and pulling Jackson on top of her. "If that's not fucking literary, I don't know what is."

The girls lay together for a while, enjoying the buzz, enjoying the desire that flowed between them, the August air too hot for them to do anything about it until later that night. "I like that new smoke," Jackson finally said. "Got a nice, sweet taste. How much did you get?"

"Enough," Taylor grinned. She thought about the kilo she had stashed up under the wheel well of the '62 Pontiac outside, about how many dime bags it would bring, how many days of not having to work the streets. "I thought you'd like it," she said, knowing how much Jackson loved the new Mexican weed coming into town. "There's still a good-size roach laying around here somewhere."

Jackson reached over to pick up the remains of the joint, clipped it, and took a long hit while Taylor held the match. "*Glistening like a tease*," she laughed, coughing on the exhale. "Girl, you are too fucking much."

Jackson

I jumped before I thought. Came around the corner, seen one brother slug her, the other pull his blade. Seen her head snap back, hit hard against the wall. Seen her knife slide away, outta reach, glistening like a tease under the sticky green dumpster. I seen her knees buckle, high heel boots crumple, pink tube top doubling over a black vinyl miniskirt. I knew right away who it was. Yeah, I been watching that one real close. Tough skinny black girl. Small, wiry, nothin' extra, nothin' wasted. Baby dreads sneaking all wild outta her cap, eyes sparking flint, a mouth could sneer your ass clear outta town or jump you so hard with a smile you forgot you had business to attend to. And that knife. Fancy pearl black handle with a mean six-inch blade. She was the quickest thing I'd ever seen with a knife that size. Some said she cut her pimp's ear off in a fight. Some said she'd Bobbitted the guy. Some said she was the one that sliced up the behind of the trick what tried to rape me my first night working in this damn town.

So, I knew better, but when I seen those punks forcing her back down the alley, her without her knife and all, I couldn't just do nothin'. So I snuck around beside the dumpster, grabbed her knife, picked up a brick, hurled it at the head of the guy who slugged her, and said something stupid like, "Hey, motherfuckers, what y'all say we make this fight a little more fair?" Well, I never seen a fight yet come down like they do in the movies, but I did manage to split open the guy's head with the brick and get that girl back her knife before something slammed across my face and I hit the pavement. When I woke up, the guys were gone, my nostrils were caked with blood and that girl was leaning over me, holding her fancy-ass knife hard against my throat.

"Well, I'm glad you finally decided to wake your sorry self up, white girl, 'cause I got some things to say to you 'bout messing round where you don't belong, messing in other people's business where you got no right to be."

I squinted up at her. "Damn," I muttered. "You're welcome."

My head hurt so bad I thought, hell, she might as well just cut if off right now and put it in that dumpster. My tongue rolled thickly around each tooth, pushing, taking inventory.

"Where'd you learn to talk so fast?" I asked.

"Shut up." She pushed the knife up under my chin. "What you think you're doing coming round here, anyway, bitch? Dragging your sorry white ass where it don't belong, riding in here like some goddamn honkey-ass cowgirl social worker, getting in the way of my personal affairs."

"Personal affairs?" I had to laugh. "Those motherfuckers were gonna *do* you, girl."

"Yeah, and what you think they gonna do to me now? Besides, I had it under control." She looked away, picking at her thumbnail with her knife.

"Yeah. Well, darlin', I'd hate to be around when you *don't* got it under control," I said. I tried not to grin and noticed her mouth fighting it, too, so I sat up real slow and easy and reached out my hand. "My name's Taylor," I said. "I'm kinda new in town."

"I know who you are," she said, putting down her knife to shake my hand. "Who do you think it was saved your sorry white ass from that motherfuckin' trick last month?"

"Damn, I *knew* that was you what cut that fool up so bad. I'd say he's the one with the truly sorry white ass, though," I laughed.

She smiled. "Yeah, well, let's just say I gave him a little something to think about. Like every time he tries to sit down, for example. Or take something he ain't paid for."

We stayed for a few more moments, laughing at the image of the john explaining his sliced-up behind to his doctor, his wife. Then I moved to get up. "Well, I better be going," I said.

My nose was starting to bleed again. I had no idea where I was gonna sleep that night. I figured by now all the good boxes would be taken out behind Montgomery Wards.

She looked away quick. "Hey, bitch. I'm serious about not wanting to see your white butt around this part of town again," she said, her voice all tough and tight.

"Yeah, whatever." I felt too tired to argue anymore and started walking away.

"But that don't mean I might not be wanting to see it in some *other* part of town," she called out, pausing. "*If* you know what I mean."

I turned around to see her standing there grinning at me under the streetlight, looking way too fine for someone who just got beat up. "I think I just might," I smiled, feeling my stomach flip over, hit down by my boots, and bounce back up around my chest again.

"Good," she said. "My name's Jackson."

we are the tiny chewed nails

we are the tiny chewed nails of a small child's hands. we always grow, give willingly to the hunger, though we are never enough to fill. and sometimes we bleed, but never enough to be bandaged. we never scratch, and have never hurt a woman or a child.

if you want to know more, go ask the mouth why she is so damn hungry.

Too Damn Easy

Taylor let go of the hammer and smiled at the way the rough leather holder caught it snug and easy. One day she'd have herself a real tool belt, but for now her old cut-up Lone Ranger cowboy holster was working just fine. She liked how the hammer felt bumping against her leg, perfectly within reach, leaving her hands free to do whatever they needed. Right now they rested squarely on bony adolescent hips as she surveyed her work, head cocked, eyes narrowed, lips pursed. "Damn, you're getting good, girl!" she said out loud. Busy checking out the smooth lines of the sheetrock patch she had just fit into the side of the garage where her mom's old Chevy had landed the night before, she didn't notice Jackson walking into the garage, shaking her head.

"Girl, why are you always fixing shit up, anyway?" Jackson scooted up into the tractor tire they had stolen that afternoon. She retied the laces of her new black hi-top sneakers for the fourteenth time that day, lit a joint.

"'Cause shit always be needing fixing up, that's why," Taylor replied.

"You know your mama's just gonna be crashing right through it next time she comes home drunk," Jackson said. She paused, then added, "Which is probably tonight. Then you two gonna get in another knockdown drag-out and you'll be back out looking for some shelter. Why do you keep coming back here, anyway?"

"My mama needs me," Taylor said. "Besides, that's what that tire's for. So she hits it before she hits the wall and don't nothin' get hurt."

"Girl, I don't know why I even bother with your fool self. Walking round with that Roy Rogers gun belt strapped onto your sorry white ass."

"'Cause you love me, that's why."

Taylor knew Jackson was still sore about losing five dollars she didn't have betting that Taylor couldn't steal the sheetrock from the 24th Street construction site.

"You said you'd cop a whole sheet of that rock," Jackson had complained.

"I *did* cop a whole sheet," Taylor insisted. "I just had to bust it up a little to get it outta there. But it still counts. I still stole the whole fucking thing, didn't I?"

"Yeah, whatever."

Taylor had taken the five dollars but had been thinking all day about something nice she could do for Jackson. She took off her belt, wiped her hands on her Levi's, and said, "Come on, baby, let's go downtown."

"Do I see that look I love in your eyes?" Jackson asked.

"Yep. That's the one. Let me just go in and put on my pink shirt and we're outta here."

At the bus stop, three white boys with fresh Army haircuts called them bitches and bulldaggers. Taylor started toward them. "Save it, baby," Jackson warned, grabbing her arm. "They ain't worth your trouble. There's a hundred thousand more just like them, anyway."

Taylor flipped them off as she followed Jackson up on the bus. She was pissed that she hadn't slugged someone but she was coming to learn that Jackson was usually right about these things. Being in the world had become a whole lot sweeter but infinitely more complicated since she and Jackson had taken up together. Used to slugging first and thinking later, Taylor's head hurt trying to figure out these new rules about when to fight and when not too. "My mama says it's all about choosing your battles," Jackson had told her once. Then there was the time Jackson warned her, "My mama says it's dangerous to get too close to white people. My mama says she's afraid you're like to get me killed someday, acting the way you do."

Taylor and Jackson made their way down the aisle to their seats on the bus, Taylor scowling at the guys standing outside, still leering at them.

"Hey, bitch!" one of the GI's called out, grabbing at his crotch. "Want some of this?"

"Fuckin' nigger-loving queer," hollered another.

Taylor spit as far as she could from the window, hoping it landed on one of them. "You got that right, you motherfuckin' sorry excuse for a dildo," she yelled as the bus pulled away. Jackson gave her one of her looks but then took her hand and they sat in silence the rest of the ride.

They got off near 19th and Laurel and circled around to get a better look at their target—Roger's Outdoor World. There were two entrances, a park across the street, a nice back alley, and lots of traffic running on 19th. Their moods were improving by the moment.

"Damn, girl, this is perfect. How'd you find this place?" Jackson asked.

"I seen it last week on my way over to Cindy's and came back to check it out," Taylor said. She pointed up the street. "See where we are? She's just two blocks down on 21st, okay, so if it all goes cool then we meet over there. Otherwise, back at the lot tonight at ten, okay?"

"Cool," Jackson nodded. "But I want to eat something first. You know how this shit gives me an appetite."

Taylor grinned over at Jackson—skinny and tough, always eating like a horse, always down for an adventure.

"Wait here. I'll get us something." Taylor would do this one alone. If waiting for a bus was difficult when they were together, stealing with a black girl was virtually impossible.

Taylor crossed over to the corner market and made a big production of buying a couple of apples to cover putting sardines and cheese down her pants. "Ya got any of them green apples?" she asked the grocer when he looked her way. "You know, those Granny Smith's?" He half-nodded to her and she was able to shift the sardine can and cheese from her sleeve to her pants while he led her down the produce aisle, backs to the cameras. Taylor and Jackson ate happily under the huge sycamore tree, watching the traffic inside Roger's Outdoor World.

Pretty soon Jackson had it figured out. "See that white fool with the pimples and suit? He's the dick, okay. Let me handle him. Those other two jokers in red vests must be the manager and the clerk. I got them too. Now tell me where you need to be."

"I figure to be somewhere over near that door in sporting goods," Taylor said.

"Sporting goods? What kind of shit you be needing in sporting goods?" Jackson frowned, raising her upper lip, narrowing her eyes.

Taylor just smiled. "I got my eye on something for you, baby."

"Damn, I don't need nothing outta no sporting goods store. Unless, of course, you've got your eye on that nice black ten-speed bike over there. I could use me one of those fine things." Jackson raised her right eyebrow. "But hey, I'll just do my thing and you do yours." She finished off the last of the sardines. "C'mon. Let's do it."

"Where you gonna be?" Taylor asked.

Jackson laughed. "There's only one place for a black girl in a sporting goods store and that's in the firearms section. It just makes white people crazy to see a nigga anywhere near their guns. Those boys will be on my ass like white on rice and you can do whatever it is you're needing to do so bad you can't hardly stop grinning. Go on in and check it out and I'll come in about three or four minutes."

Taylor stood up and tucked in the pink ruffled blouse Jackson called her "white girl stealing shirt." She combed her hair, something she never did unless she was going to steal, and gave Jackson a wink and a grin. She left her the bulky jacket and headed over to Roger's Outdoor World.

"Can I help you, little lady?"

It just killed her when these fools called her "little lady" or "ma'am." *This shirt is fucking magic*, she thought to herself.

"Yes, sir. I was kind of hoping to find a nice case for my daddy's hunting knife. It's his birthday coming up." Taylor thought about Jackson's favorite knife that her brother had brought her from Ghana—the intricately carved black handle and the flashing six-inch blade that she kept so damn sharp it cut right through the oily rags she wrapped around it. Taylor had planned on getting her a fancy leather case, but now that Jackson laid down a dare on that damn ten-speed bike, there was only one thing to do.

She followed the bald head in the red vest over to the cabinet where they kept the knives and cases, noticing that the bikes were not only *not* chained together but they were also ridiculously close to the side entrance with an overhead sign reading THIS DOOR TO REMAIN UNLOCKED DURING BUSINESS HOURS.

Damn, there is a god, Taylor laughed to herself. *This is gonna be too fucking easy. It looks like there's even some air in the tires.*

"Oh, sir, I really like this one," she smiled, pointing to the black case with turquoise beadwork. She hadn't seen Jackson come in, but she could feel her presence and had noticed both the pimple-faced suit and the other red vest move quickly over to firearms.

Her bald red vest was becoming much less attentive so she figured he had spotted Jackson as well. He took out the black leather case, cradling it in soft, pudgy hands. "Now, this *is* a pretty one. You got good taste, little lady. I know your daddy would really like this one, but it will cost you quite a few weeks of allowance money."

"Oh, I've been saving up for this," Taylor crooned. Then the call came over the loudspeaker for manager assistance in the firearms section. Taylor wished she could go over and watch Jackson in action, but she knew this was her move. The red vest excused himself and said he'd let her decide.

"Thank you for all your help. I think I can take care of myself now."

It was all too easy. Taylor had the knife case in her pocket and was out the door on Jackson's new bicycle in less than a minute. She didn't think anyone was after her, but she tore through the alley down to 23rd before circling back to Cindy's garage just to be sure. Waiting for Jackson, she checked out the bike, thinking, *Damn, leave it to that girl to pick out the best damn bike in the place from two hundred yards away.*

"Nice bike." Jackson was leaning up against the door, smiling.

Taylor blushed, startled. "I got it for you, baby."

"They just made that too damn easy," Jackson said. "My mama always said fools be so busy watching out for black folks that they never see the white ones robbing them blind."

"I'm not sure this is exactly what your mama had in mind." Taylor laughed.

"Yeah, whatever. It works. Anyway, I got something for you too, baby." Jackson pulled something out from under her jacket and handed it to Taylor.

"Hot damn, it's a fucking tool belt," Taylor exclaimed. "It's beautiful! Check out this leather. I gotta steal me some more tools for all these little holders. What you think goes in here? How the hell did you get this out?"

"Well, those three boys were so busy chasing some skinny white girl on a bicycle down the street, I just figured, what the hey, and helped myself." Jackson paused. "Probably shoulda gotten me a gun while I was at it."

"You're the best."

"Yeah, guess I am."

the mother sucks
the baby's marrow

the mother sucks the baby's marrow out of her existence. the baby curls into her pain, fetal, futile. body closed, eyes closed, mouth closed in toothless grip on tiny pink thumb, feeding herself. little mouth sucking sounds like puppies on a teat. the young girl gnaws her nails down low, biting torn and crooked bits and spitting them away. "I AM NOT GIRL. I AM NOT PRETTY." eyes glaring. mouth working like a wolf caught in a cold steel trap, leaving its leg behind. the woman's mouth, too, reaches for fingers and nails. a lineage of pain eating at the hunger. because mouths don't think about what it is they're doing. because mouths reach blind for whatever is at hand.

like a woman

The other girls tell me I am going to have to dress like a woman if I'm going to make it on the street. "Screw you." I laugh. "I've been fucked all my life and I've never had to wear a dress yet."

"Just tryin' to help you out, girl," they call out as they walk on down Santa Monica Boulevard, ankles bowed out over wobbly spike heels, popping their gum and adjusting their spaghetti-strap bras as if they had something special going on down there. Don't none of us 'cept Lisa have any tits yet, and even if I had 'em I wasn't about to go dressin' in no drag shit. For one thing, it costs too much and I've got better things to do with my money. And for another thing I can't hardly walk in that shit, much less run. Or fight. Some girls can, though. I seen one girl whip off those fuck-me pumps and bust some motherfucker trying to get something for nothing across the side of his head quicker than I could have cracked his nuts. Said she fucked up his eardrum 'cause she got the pointy part right inside his earhole and see, check out that blood, girl. I think she was just feeling good 'cause she got his wallet, messed him up and didn't even break a heel.

It was good for me, 'cause she made a buy with the joker's money. That was before I was living on the streets. I just came down to deal, mostly pot but sometimes opium and acid. You had to carry if you wanted to run the serious shit and it wasn't my style. They all laughed and called me Mahatma 'cause I was always reading Gandhi and Thoreau and shit about nonviolence and revolution and civil disobedience, but we was all tight anyway. We watched each other's backs and they knew I could fight like a motherfuckin' crazy person if I got pushed too far or somebody I hung out with was being messed up. There was no doubt but that I'd kill somebody if I had a gun, so it was better to just stick to dealing pot and reading my books. I had a lot of reading to do.

So, yeah, now I'm working the trade. I didn't particularly want to but there aren't exactly a lot of career opportunities for fifteen-year-old girls living on the streets of L.A. The truth is, I was getting fucked anyway so I figured I might as well get paid for it, right? You couldn't sleep anywhere without waking up to find some guy's dick poking around looking for some hole, didn't matter which one. Seems like ever since I can remember I been waking up to find some big hairy thing climbing on or off of me. I got tired of it and thought, hell, I can't get any sleep anyway, I'm going to make somebody pay for this shit. At least now I'm calling the shots and making some money. And I was right. Don't need no fancy drag dress. There is plenty of trade. I do all right. Lots of hairy guys just dying to pay for bait. Tell me I remind them of their daughter and then tell me how they want me to fuck them. They got some messed-up shit, man, but the money's good. Better than working at McDonalds, right?

The White Girl

The white girl seems unaware of how the men are looking at her. That's the first thing I notice about her. She does not engage the eyes of the men. Unless, of course, they are looking for drugs. A friend of Trina's, the white girl comes down to the boulevard to deal. She feeds only the hunger for the drugs; ignores the other hungers, ignores the eyes that want her. The fact that she is not soliciting the men makes them want her even more.

I see everything, even myself—a black girl watching the white girl ignoring the men who are watching her, wanting her. I spit and gently finger my knife. There is something slightly dangerous about this skinny white girl who strides the streets in her heavy boots and possible ignorance, half looking like she owns the territory, half looking like she's just landed from another planet. "Jackson, baby, you just leave that white girl be," my mama warns me. "White girl like that like to get you killed."

We know it's just a matter of time before the white girl can no longer ignore the eyes of the men and soon she too is selling more than drugs. I watch the eyes of the men in the Pontiacs, Chryslers, and Fords cruise slowly by, watching the girls who pretend to not be watching them. Sometimes the car slows in front of the black girl and I take a long last drag off my cigarette, straighten my tube top and walk over to the open passenger window, clicking the heels of my boots hard against the pavement, determined to make this white man pay for his desire. I watch it all, even as I feel the white boots pinch my feet, even as I smell the booze, aftershave, and lust pour out the trick's open window.

Sometimes the car slows in front of Trina, Francine, or Jo-Jo—the Puerto Rican, white, and half-Chinese girls. "We've got all the flavors right here on this one block," Trina laughs, calling out to the men. All the girls are young; all the men are not. Sometimes the car slows in front of the strange new white girl and the other girls suck their teeth and frown. "What they want her for anyway?" they complain. "She don't even look like a girl."

The white girl never wears dresses, never wears heels or makeup. I watch her close. She keeps to herself, fights at the drop of a dime. Fights like a pit bull. Uses her fists as well as her palm. Kicks those heavy black boots fierce and quick as hooves. Keeps an easy grip on her knife, says, "Come on, motherfucker, come on in." Her hands are strong; nails chewed to the quick. I see everything. The white girl stands on the corner with her striped t-shirt tight against her small breasts, her hands shoved deep into the pockets of her black jeans. And the men slow down, circle back around.

"Oh, she's a girl, all right," I tell the others. "Even though she doesn't dress much like one." The men want her because they can see she doesn't want them and yet still they get to have her. That kind of desire cannot be contained. And the white girl makes them pay for their desire, even as she struggles to maintain control over it.

For she does not understand their desire, has not yet learned to use it against them. She only knows to fight or yield. The white girl is tough as nails, but my mama is right—there's a lot she doesn't know. My mama says, "Only white folks can walk around that ignorant and survive. A black girl that arrogant and that ignorant, she'd be dead in a week."

One day I see the white girl pinned up against the wall behind the 7-11, some john trying to steal what he should be paying for. The white girl's head is bleeding, nodding forward and then back against the brick wall. Her knife is gone. I take mine out from my boot and look around. Trina crosses the street to stand guard and cover me. "You gonna do him?" she asks.

"Nah," I tell her. "I'm just gonna wake him up a little. Leave my mark."

I slice up the behind of the trick that's gotten out of control. He yelps in pain, drops the white girl, reaches back to his bleeding ass and stares in disbelief at his dripping hands. Then I'm gone, watching from the corner. The white girl comes to enough to crush the heel of her palm up into the man's nose, breaking it easy. As he bends down in pain, she lifts her knee up into his head and he tumbles over. For a moment she stands there looking lost, confused. At this point she could either run or harm, but clearly she cannot remember the rules that govern those decisions. Finally, the white girl pulls cash from the man's wallet and walks away, spitting blood.

When in doubt, steal. I laugh to myself. That white girl loves to steal. Everywhere she goes, everything she does, she's gotta take something with her. Me, I prefer to leave my mark, leave something behind for them to remember me by. My mama says when I was little she'd have to whip me for always writing in other people's books. "But Mama," I'd tell her, "I've got something to say, too." And I know that trick is going to remember my mark on his behind a lot longer than he will the few hundred dollars the white girl stole from him. I like to leave my mark. That's why I want to write. The white girl, she's just trying to get back something that was taken from her a long time ago. My mama says the white girl's a fool, says you can't ever get back what's been taken. You just gotta go on and make your way in the world.

My mama says that white girl's nothing but trouble, tells me to stay away from her.

But I don't. I watch for her. My heart catches when I see her body coil for a fight. My stomach dips when she catches my eye, looks down at my knife, curls her lip. Then one day she steps into a bad situation where three guys have me cornered in an alley, trying to make me pay for something my brother did or did not do. She jumps right into the fight, hollers, "Hey motherfuckers," slides me back my knife and busts open one guy's head and cuts another before she gets knocked out. Saves my life. I sit with her after it's all over, waiting for her to come to. She'll never make it through the night if I leave her, a girl alone in this part of town, unconscious. My mama says, "Get on out of there, girl, before those boys come back for you," but I stay, holding my knife in one hand, hers in the other.

I've never seen the white girl up so close before. Her hair is wild; curls lie matted in blood against her forehead. I watch her breasts rise and fall; her belly is tight and flat, her long legs muscular and lean, black jeans tucked into her boots. I imagine what it would be like to lay alongside such length, wonder how my body would fit up against hers. Then she stirs and I jump back, kneel down and press my knife up against her throat.

The white girl lies still, respecting the knife but showing no fear. "Damn," she says. "You're welcome." She tries to smile, but her mouth is swollen and bloody "I know you," she says, shifting her body slightly, stretching out her legs. "You're the one that cut up the behind of the trick what tried to rape me that night."

It excites me to see the white girl lie still beneath the knife but show no fear. I send her away but then dream of her length, dream of her flashing green eyes, her cocky grin. Weeks go by and I do not see the white girl, not even down on the boulevard. Then one day, there she is, leaning up against the wall, talking to Trina, her Levi jacket and a duffle bag hanging over one shoulder. She watches me cross the street and walk toward them. She looks down at the right boot where I keep my knife and I open my hands and smile. She nods.

"Girlfriend needs a place to stay," Trina says, hiding a grin. "Got any ideas?"

The white girl follows me home. We cut across the railroad tracks, up through the fields behind the power plant to a three-acre lot filled with wrecked cars. A huge Rottweiler comes lunging toward us, leaping up against the cyclone fence. "Hey, J. Edgar," I call softly. "Good to see you, boy."

I see everything. I watch myself lead through a tear in the fencing, tying it back up with a piece of wire. "Stand still," I tell the white girl. "Let him smell you." The dog snarls. The white girl stands still and easy, turns her head slightly away, dropping her hand, showing no fear. And my breath catches and I know that Mama's wrong, that the white girl's courage is a real thing, not just stupidity. Soon J. Edgar trots at the white girl's side, showing her the way. She is the first person, besides me and my brother, that J. Edgar has let into this yard.

The camper on the wrecked Ford three-quarter-ton pickup is where I mostly live, but we climb inside the back of the totaled black stretch limousine. The front of the car has been crashed in, the engine pushed up into the driver's seat. But the middle is untouched and this is where I take the white girl. The sinks in the wet bar are dry and the television and phones don't work, but the leather seats are fine and the couch is big enough for two to sleep on. The white girl grins, sets her bag down, takes off her boots, and leans back onto the couch. I can't tell if she knows what's she's doing or hasn't got a clue but I slide in next to her, and she pulls me all up against her, her face in my neck, her arms strong around my back, her hands and her body moving like they know exactly what they're doing.

I didn't mean to take up with a white girl and lord knows it ain't easy. She's dangerous—Mama's right about that. And ignorant. I've never seen someone so ignorant. I even have to teach her how to put grease in my hair. "Haven't you ever had a black girlfriend before?" I ask her.

She smiles. "I ain't never had any kind of girlfriend before," she says, reaching for the oil, pulling me down in front of her.

The white girl's different, that's for sure. I come home one day and find her laying across J. Edgar, pinning him on his back. She's got her teeth into his neck, growling, shaking him slightly and growling some more till he finally lies totally still. Then she lets go, says, "Okay, boy, you can get up now." J. Edgar gets up, wiggling like a puppy, wagging his tail and licking the white girl's hand. "It's an alpha dog thing," she says. "We're like a family now. You let a ninety-pound Rottweiler be head of your pack and you've got trouble."

I laugh, taking the white girl down, growling into her neck. "I let *you* be head of the pack and we've got some *serious* trouble," I tell her, and she lays still, trembling with everything but fear.

rotten

rotten teeth. rotten attitude. rotten life. so what. just another bad kid with a bad mouth. holes no one dares to notice, much less cares to fill. and the old, rotting bodies simply see me smile. yes. see me smile. see what you want to see. while i live out the difference.

nothin' but trouble

So, you wanna know where we live. Well, which home you want to hear about first? Our oceanfront property? The garden estate? Perhaps our in-town residence? Or maybe the gated community—private, fenced, patrolled by a top-of-the-line security service.

Yeah, I'll show you that one first. Me and Jackson, we got two main residences there, one primarily for entertainment purposes and one for just daily living. Come on, I'll show you.

The side entrance is the one we mostly use, on the east side down by the railroad tracks where the chain-link fence has been bolt cut and then wired back together. You can't hardly see it unless you know what you're looking for, but even then you'd be so busy stumbling back from the ninety-pound Rottweiler hurling himself up against the fence, his snarling spit splashing across your face so bad, that trying to *open* that side entrance would be the last thing on your mind. The dog? That would be J. Edgar, our own private security service. J. Edgar don't let nobody in except us. Me and J. Edgar, we had to work a few things out from the jump, but now that dog will roll right over for me, give me his throat.

Anyway, once J. Edgar lets you in, which he won't, you gotta go down this *row*, or I should say *pile*, of Plymouths, past the cherry picker and the shed of engine blocks, out toward the back of the yard. Over there on the left, that's the stretch limo, crashed in front and back, but still good in the middle—got these wide leather seats, soft, creamy white like a bed, curled all around like a half-circle moon. Then there's the wet bar, which I don't got hooked up yet to water, but I'm gonna, and the refrigerator, which I got wired to the battery of a Cutlass Supreme. There's lights, too, but we can't ever turn 'em on, of course. So that's our entertainment residence. Not that we ever have anybody that comes over, but me and Jackson, we find our own damn selves pretty entertaining, if you know what I mean.

Now our main residence is that old three-quarter-ton Ford stepside over there. Primer grey, windshield busted, driver's side door gone, seats stripped, rusted out clear through the floorboards. My daddy used to say Ford stood for "fix or repair daily," said Fords would bring you nothin' but trouble. Guess he'd know because he worked on 'em for years. But we don't need that thing to run; we just need it to hold up the camper shell on its back.

Ever since Jackson took me in, that's where we mostly live. Jackson painted the outside with all them signs you see. Don't ask me what they mean. All that red, green, black—they just something her grandma taught her, marks to keep folks away, white folks mostly, I guess. Didn't work too good with me, though. Jackson said, once she seen me, her mama, she just shook her head, said it's been known for one to sometimes slip through, said only her god knows why and he ain't telling. Jackson's mama, she don't like me too much, even though I did save her daughter's life. She says a white girl can't mean nothing but trouble, says I'ma like to get her baby killed, says I'm just one more damn cross for an old woman to bear.

Anyway, aside from me, them old Africa marks do a pretty good job of keeping folks away from us. It probably don't hurt none either that J. Edgar has made his bed underneath this particular truck, or that this is where he gets tied up when men come into the yard to look for parts. Besides, there ain't hardly nothing left to take. This old truck's been picked clean as a chicken bone. The engine's gone, so we leave the hood propped up so everyone can see there ain't nothing but a hole gaping inside. A hole just like the socket in Jackson's mouth where her tooth used to be before that john tried to rearrange her face last week. I know he got the worst of it, guess she cut him up pretty bad, probably removing somethin' of his body parts if I know Jackson. Now, Jackson, she ain't like me, she don't like to fight, but you just try and mess with that girl's face and she'll cut you quicker than you can spit. That black, pearl-handled knife just flies around like it's got a life of its own. She especially don't like nobody messing with her mouth; that girl's serious as a heart attack about those perfect teeth, makes me steal her Colgate extra fluoride, mint floss, and a brand new toothbrush every few weeks, brushes like five times a day, even when we don't hardly got nothing to eat. And that girl don't never, and I mean never, give head or lip lock with a trick. Yeah, she's fierce about her mouth. Like right now she's standing there, acting all like a realtor, showing you our home with me, but inside I see she's got her tongue searching around, interrogating that hole, and I just know that someday, some way, somebody's gonna pay.

Anyway, this is where we live...maybe tomorrow we'll go check out our oceanfront property and you can see how the light from the twenty-four-hour Chevron sign shines down at just the right angle into the drain pipes off Venice Beach and you can just curl up in there, listen to the howling surf, and read as late as you want with no one bothering you. As long as the weather's dry, of course. And you got J. Edgar to watch your back.

the mouth screams on

the mouth screams on till i no longer hear. red lips curling hateful till i no longer feel. mouth distorted, smearing like a nightmare taking shape. out of the mouth comes the thick grey smoke surrounding my face no matter how i turn. out of the mouth come the pearl-brown teeth that sit in a jar on the bedstand all night long. sometimes i see them move. out of the mouth comes the racking cough, the phlegm pulled up from weary lungs that no longer hold together. out of the mouth come the strings of yellow vomit cigarettes and a whiskey sour, spewing out so loud i think she's gonna die. and all i really want to know is what happened to the kisses.

Dear Mama

Dear Mama,

It's Tuesday noon. Taylor hasn't come home yet. The sun's beating down on this metal roof something fierce. Taylor said she could get us some kind of green plastic roofing and build us some shade, but I told her we can't have this place looking like anything other than a broken-down camper. She said "Yeah" and got real quiet like she does and then said, "Yeah, well, but that don't mean we can't cool it off on the inside, now does it?" She says she might know how to get us some power, at least hook up a fan and maybe that old cooler so we don't have to keep hauling ice. Last night she went and borrowed us a battery from that wrecked Pontiac Firebird Jimmy just hauled in. Now she's out getting some wiring, and, if I know Taylor, probably also stealing a book to tell her how to do it. You just don't ever know with Taylor what she really knows and what she says she knows, but you can always count on her figuring something out.

I know, Mama, you don't like her stealing. I know you think she's nothing but trouble for me, but her and Jimmy and J. Edgar, they're like my family now, at least in the flesh. But Mama, I worry about Jimmy. He's doing good, all clean now, running his business.

But ever since he started hanging with the Panthers, working in that free breakfast program, the police have been all over this place. I don't understand, Mama. When he was dealing dope, they left him alone, but now that he's clean and doing something good, they're here all the time, shaking him down, rousting his car, sitting across the street watching him. It scares me, Mama. And Jimmy, he can't talk to you like I can, so I don't even know how he gets by.

Mama, when you died, a hole opened up so big I just fell in, screaming, crying like a baby, and when you wouldn't let me go with you, me and the world, we just turned each other inside out and now that hole is deep inside me, a screaming tear right where my heart's supposed to be. I don't know how to be in this world without you, Mama, and you won't let me come be with you, so what am I supposed to do? I know the white girl's trouble, Mama, you didn't raise no fool, but she also saved my life. That girl's got my back, and you know she treats me good. That white girl'd risk her life for me, Mama. I know, I know—*if* she don't get me killed first.

Like that time she tried to teach me how to ride freight trains and I wouldn't go with her up to Santa Barbara where she knew the yard, knew the bulls, knew the tracks. "There's trains right here," I said. "Why do we have to go up to Santa Barbara? You know that town's crawling with white people." And she said, "Yeah, well, I just ain't never caught a train here before. But, hell, we can try." And we watched and she asked the bums and we hid from the bulls and then this long silver train came sliding real slow down the tracks and Taylor said, "Okay, this is it, remember what I told you," and we ran toward an empty boxcar with its door cracked open and I caught a good grip and swung myself up just like she said and a minute later she came tumbling in after me and the train picked up speed and we crawled up against some packing blankets and she turned and I leaned back into her, her legs gripping my hips, and the train was rumbling faster and faster and her arms were wrapped tight around my chest and the hole in my heart was filled with our laughter and for once the screams were silent.

Of course, then the blankets moved on the other side of the boxcar and we both jumped up with our knives, scaring the pants off some old orange-headed guy with a bottle and a nasty-looking beard. "Whatchu doing here?" Taylor hollered out, making her voice all low like she does when she is scared or wants to sound like a man.

"I'm sleeping, or trying to," said the guy. "What are you two doing here?"

I watched Taylor relax her grip on the knife, lowering it back toward her boot. She knows how to read crazy white people better than I do, so I followed her lead. "We're heading north," she said. "Gonna jump just outside of Pajaro when the train slows down." Then the man coughed and spit out his wine laughing and that's how we found out not only were we not headed north, but we'd somehow hopped on the Grey Ghost, a train which the old guy said did not stop or slow till it got to Texas.

Now, Mama, I know you know what happened next, because I called your name more times in the next forty-eight hours than a girl should in a lifetime. Called it soft and low as we stood in the doorway watching the tough desert ground rush past in a night blur; called it screaming loud as we jumped into the dawn sky when the damn train finally slowed for a grade; called it cursing as we walked the ten miles toward what the old guy thought might be the direction of a town; and Mama, I called it in desperate prayer as we hid in corners, dumpsters, and finally curled inside a dryer of an all-night Laundromat, running from the three white town boys with baseball bats, chasing us down, calling, "Hey kitty, kitty, kitty, here pussy, pussy, pussy, hey nigger, nigger, nigger."

Next morning Taylor snuck out to a café and talked a truck driver into giving us a ride out of there. Yeah, Mama, talking wasn't all she did to convince him, but hey, she got us back home, didn't she?

Anyway, I gotta go now, Mama. I hear J. Edgar barking and I think Taylor might be back. We'll see if she can get that fan working, cool things off a little. Just give Taylor a chance, okay, Mama? You know she cares about me. You know there's a lot worse out there. I know she's a mess, Mama, but hey, like you always say, maybe that white girl like to get me killed, but she sure as hell ain't gonna get me pregnant.

Tricks

Taylor climbed up into the camper, slapping her thigh and calling to J. Edgar. "Come on, boy! Come on up." The huge Rottweiler jumped in, skidding on the slippery linoleum floor, happy to be allowed inside.

"Girl, get that damn dog outta here," Jackson complained. "He's all dirty. Besides, you know Jimmy doesn't like it when you let him off the chain."

"Ah, it's almost closing time," Taylor said, shutting the door. "Nobody's gonna steal nothing now. Besides, we've been working on some new tricks, haven't we, boy?" She pulled J. Edgar into her side, rubbing his ears. "Come on, let's show off what you can do."

Jackson sighed, put down her pen, closed up her journal. "Okay," she said, sitting up and swinging her legs off the bed. "Show me what you two fools have done now."

"Here," Taylor said. She handed Jackson a freshly rolled joint. "This should make things even more entertaining." She held the light, took one nice hit for herself, and then turned to J. Edgar. "Okay, boy. You ready?"

J. Edgar wiggled in anticipation, ears perking up when Taylor reached for the treats.

"Sit," Taylor said. J. Edgar promptly sat, alert, head high. "Good boy. Now, lie down." The dog threw his body down into a lying-down position and Taylor tossed him a treat, laughing. "He gets kind of enthusiastic about his tricks when there's food involved."

"What's that you're giving him?" Jackson asked. "It looks nasty."

"Just some Gaines Burgers, crumbled up. It ain't nasty. It's what I used to feed all my dogs when I was a kid." She smiled at J. Edgar, still holding his down position. "Besides, it's the easiest five-fingered discount they got."

Jackson took another hit. "Can you make him play dead?"

"Nah." Taylor frowned and shook her head. "But watch this. J. Edgar, belly up!" The dog rolled over onto his back, legs bent, throat and belly exposed. "Good boy," Taylor said. "Okay, buddy, roll over!" She made a small circle in the air with her finger and J. Edgar rolled completely over, coming back up into a classic belly-on-the-ground, full alert down position, looking like he could spring into action at a moment's notice. She tossed him a treat. She asked for eye contact and then gave him his next command. "J. Edgar, chill out!"

Jackson laughed as the big dog threw himself over onto his side, stretched his legs full out, and closed his eyes. "Ha! That's the best one," she said.

"Nah, you ain't even seen the best," Taylor said. "Watch this." She asked J. Edgar for a sit and then said, "Okay, boy, gimme five!"

J. Edgar raised a massive paw and slapped it down on her outstretched palm.

"Good boy!" Taylor pointed over to Jackson. "Now, give her a wave." She gave the dog her hand signal and J. Edgar picked up his paw and held it straight out in the air. It was more like a salute than a wave, but she tossed him a treat anyway, smiling. "Yeah, we gotta work a little more on that trick. Okay, last one." She sat down on the bed next to Jackson and kissed her quickly on the neck. "Baby, I think you're really gonna like this next one," she said.

J. Edgar was still in his sit position, staring at her, waiting.

"Paw up!" Taylor said, and the dog threw his front leg straight out into the air. Taylor tried not to laugh at the serious intensity of the muscle-bound Rottie, body coiled tight, face in full frown concentration as he watched for her next command. "Hold it..." Taylor said. She leaned over and whispered in Jackson's ear, "Watch close now.

"J. Edgar," she said, locking eyes with him. "Are you gay?"

Body tight, front leg still held stiff out in the air, J. Edgar relaxed his wrist joint so just his paw went suddenly limp, dropping down at a rakish angle. The two girls fell out laughing and J. Edgar took advantage of the moment to help himself to the last of the Gaines Burger patties.

"Girl, you are too damn foolish," Jackson laughed, pushing Taylor away. "You two need to go off and join some damn circus. You all are too much. My mama always says that California white people and their dogs are just a special kind of crazy. Now go on and get that filthy dog out of my camper before Jimmy sees him gone and gets all mad."

Taylor laughed and rubbed J. Edgar's ears. "You're a good dog. A real good dog." She opened the camper door and gestured for him to jump down. "Now go on out there and protect us, buddy. Protect us from the world."

Cross Pen

Taylor made her way down the rows of wrecked cars and spotted Jackson curled up in the back seat of the totaled gold Cadillac, lost in thought. The two girls had a running joke about how they each knew all the other's favorite hangout places in the sprawling two-acre junkyard, Jackson preferring the Caddys, limos, and Benzes with their wood-grained dashboards and plushy interiors. Taylor tended toward old trucks and station wagons, or, her all-time favorite, the tops of the piles of flattened cars, stacked seven high and waiting for scrap metal pickup. Without speaking, without having to tell where they'd be, the girls could sense each other's whereabouts, taking great pleasure in finding each other, and in being found.

Taylor crouched down and leaned her arms on the open passenger side window of the '69 Coup de Ville. "Hey, baby." She grinned.

Jackson looked up and smiled. She put down her writing pad and reached toward Taylor. "Hey, girlfriend," she said. "Door's busted, but come on in."

Taylor climbed through the window and slid in alongside Jackson. Half lying on the soft leather seats, she wrapped her arms around the girl and nuzzled into her neck, kissing that sweet side hollow just above the collarbone where the tiny dreadlocks barely touched.

Jackson let out a soft moan. "Yeah, girl, you know *exactly* where to find me. That's no lie." She pushed Taylor's wild mass of hair out of their faces and let her hand linger at the nape of the girl's neck, still slightly damp from the hot trek back from town. Gently, she pulled Taylor's head back a little. "Let me see your eyes, baby. You got something for me?"

Taylor buried her face deeper into her lover's shoulder. "Yeah, I got a little something for you," she growled, trying to make her voice all low and sexy.

Jackson punched her in the shoulder and pushed her away, laughing. "You *know* that's not what I meant," she said. "I mean, did you bring me what I needed from town?"

Taylor sat up and reached into her jacket pocket. "I had to go clear 'cross town to the fancy stores, but I found just what you asked for." She opened her hand. "A brand-new, shiny gold Cross pen, just like you wanted. Top of the line. Hell, for what they're trying to sell this shit for…"

"Taylor," Jackson interrupted. "What do you mean, *a brand-new pen?*"

"What do you mean, what do I mean?" Taylor said. "I mean I stole you a brand-new pen, exactly like your other one. That's what you wanted, right?" Starting to panic, Taylor ran a quick mental search for what could possibly be wrong this time. *Jackson's pen ran outta ink. Girl can't stand to write with anything other than that damn fancy-ass Cross pen, so I take my sorry butt all the way 'cross town, find the fancy-ass store that sells the damn things, con the high-heeled bitch behind the counter that's looking at me like I'm a piece of shit, still make the swipe clean, don't draw no heat, get back here in less than two hours with the damn pen, so what the fuck? Damn. A minute ago I was all tight in her arms, feeling fine, and now she's looking like somebody died, or like she don't even want to know me anymore.*

Jackson shook her head and sighed. "Damn, Taylor, I didn't need a new goddamn pen. I just needed a new ink cartridge for the pen I had." She reached out her hand. "Here, let me see that thing."

Taylor handed her the pen and leaned back against the passenger door, arms crossed, hating that too-familiar sinking feeling like everything was about to turn real bad. "What do you mean, 'cartridge'?" she asked. "You didn't say nothing about no damn cartridges."

Jackson examined the pen, turning it over in her hands. "I said my pen was running out of ink," she said, her voice low and measured. "I thought you knew what that meant." She unscrewed the top of the pen and pulled out the inside cartridge. "See," she explained. "That's all you needed to get. Just the replacement cartridge. Not the whole stupid pen. Damn, girl. Why you always gotta make everything so complicated?"

Taylor snorted. "Yeah, right. Like *I'm* the one making shit complicated! I cop you an expensive-ass pen, exactly like your other one, and suddenly, instead of saying thank you, you're getting all in my face and calling me stupid. What the fuck!"

"Taylor. I didn't say you were stupid. It's just that everybody knows you don't have to get a whole brand-new damn pen every time you run out of ink. Shit."

Now Taylor was really pissed. "Yeah, well obviously *every*body don't know *every*thing about everything. How the fuck am I supposed to know about some goddamn *replacement cartridge*? I ain't never even seen a pen like this before, until I seen you writing with yours. Nobody I ever knew even had this kind of shit. You just had a simple goddamn nineteen-cent pen and when it ran out of ink you tossed it and bought or five-fingered another." Taylor leaned her head back out the window, closed her eyes, and took a deep breath. "Damn," she said. "Why we fighting, anyway?"

The two girls sat in uneasy silence on opposite sides of the car. Overhead, the power lines hummed, and across the tracks the freeway noise droned on, broken by an occasional siren. Flies buzzed against the rear windshield, bumping into the glass, looking for a way out. Finally, Jackson spoke. "I didn't grow up with this shit either," she said, her voice soft.

"I know you didn't," Taylor said. "So I guess I just don't see what the big fuckin' deal is. Seems like the more expensive something is, the more hassle comes with it, if you ask me."

She slapped at one of the smaller flies buzzing by her ear. *Girl, just let it go,* she told herself. *Just let it lie and you'll figure it all out later.* But she couldn't, and before she knew it, her mouth was back in action.

"Besides," she started up again, turning toward Jackson, "why *you* trippin', anyway? I'm the one that took my sorry ass clear across town to do something nice for you, sucking smog in this stinkin' heat, making three damn bus changes, going into a store where people looked at me like I was a piece of shit they wished they could wipe off their shoes, and I still figured out a way to steal you a brand-new goddamn fancy-ass pen, exactly like the one that ran outta ink. So what if I didn't know about the goddamn ink cartridges. You still got a brand new fucking pen. With a new fucking ink cartridge. So, why you gotta ride my ass for what I didn't do just perfect?" Taylor paused. "Damn. It's too hot to deal with this shit. I'll catch you later." She started to climb back out the side window.

"Wait," Jackson said. "Don't go." She reached out and touched Taylor's shoulder, pulling her back into the car. "Listen, you're right. I am tripping. I'm sorry. I just got scared, that's all. You're right. It ain't no big deal." She held out the new pen, unscrewing the top for the second time. "Look, just give me back my old pen. I'll put this new pen's cartridge in it and it will be good as new. We'll even have us an extra backup pen and next time we're downtown we can get some extra cartridges. Listen, girl. I'm sorry I went off on you like that. I just tripped, that's all. Gimme my pen. It's cool."

Taylor felt the sick feeling rise up again. She wished she could just go back to having her face buried in Jackson's neck, both of them laughing, her heart busting clear out of her chest it was so full, back when everything was okay. That moment felt like a lifetime ago. Now, the only way out was to go on through. She forced herself to look up at Jackson. "I don't have your pen anymore."

"What the hell you mean you don't have my pen anymore?" Jackson said, grabbing Taylor's shirt. "Girl, where's my goddamn pen! Please do not tell me you threw away my Cross pen."

"Nah, baby, I didn't throw it away. I had to leave it at the store. Baby, I'm sorry. I had to swap for the new one when they wasn't looking. That's the only way I could make the cop."

"You left my pen at the store?" Jackson's jaw clenched. "Damn, fool. Why the fuck would you leave my pen at the goddamn store? What the hell were you thinking?"

"Baby, I'm telling you, it's the only way I could make the cop. You don't know what those stores are like. They got that goddamn shit locked up like Fort Knox. Everything's in these locked glass display cases. You can't touch nothing. You gotta get the manager to open the shit up and then they be watching your ass so tight you can't even think about making a move. And that part of town's screaming with rich people and rent-a-cops so I knew I couldn't pull a snatch-and-dash. Hell no. I wouldn't even know which way to run. So it was all I could do to just stand there and bullshit my way through until the bitch glanced away for a second to sign for a delivery and I could make the switch. It was real clean. I just slid the pen up my sleeve and put your old one back into the fancy box in a flash and told them I'd have to think about whether or not I wanted the gold or silver one and I'd be back…"

"Ah, shut up, Taylor. I don't want to listen to another one of your stupid stealing stories. Hell, girl, you steal even when you don't got to. How stupid is that?"

"I said don't call me stupid," Taylor growled. "Besides, what am I not getting? Look, I'm sorry about your pen, but the one I got you is exactly the same, except it's brand new. That's better, right? What's so fucking special about that particular pen, anyway?"

Taylor watched the vein in Jackson's forehead pulse, her jaw clenching and releasing. "My mama gave me that pen."

"Ah, shit." Taylor punched the padded doorframe with her fist. "Damn, why didn't you tell me that pen came from your mama?"

Jackson just looked out the window. "She gave it to me the day I graduated from high school. She said she knew I was going to make my mark on the world and that she wanted to be a part of it in some small way. I know it musta taken her a week's worth of wages to save up for that damn pen."

"Wait. You graduated from high school? What the fuck. Why didn't you ever tell me you graduated from high school?"

"Because I didn't want to make you feel bad. I know how you trip on anything to do with education. Look, it ain't about that anyway. It ain't about me telling or not telling you shit. It's about you fucking up and losing my mama's pen. *Why* didn't I tell you about the cartridges? *Why* didn't I tell you about my mama giving me the pen? Hell, I couldn't possibly even think fast enough to imagine everything I'd have to tell you so you didn't go off and do something stupid." Jackson sighed. "Look. Just forget it. Just go, okay."

"No problem. I'm outta here." Taylor crawled back out through the window. "Goddamn motherfucking piece of shit," she cursed, slamming her fist on the trunk of the Caddy. She kicked out the side windows of three Chevys as she made her way down the row of cars and back out into the street. J. Edgar wisely kept his distance, watching from the shade of a totaled Plymouth.

When Taylor returned, it was dusk and she found Jackson sitting on the hood of a '65 Mustang, knees curled up to her chest.

"Hey girl," Jackson called softly. "Glad you came back."

"Look," Taylor started. "I'm sorry…"

"Nah, girl, I'm sorry. I'm sorry I called you stupid. I'm sorry I went off on you like that."

"No, it's my fault. I blew it. I shoulda known about those damn cartridges."

Jackson shook her head. "My mama says you can only know what you know and there ain't no shame in that."

"Yeah, well that could save me a hell of a lot of shame, because what I don't know could fill up a dumpster ten times over. Anyway, I'm sorry. I brought you something." She handed Jackson a white shopping bag, wrapped in red ribbon. "Open it."

"Sunset Stationers?" Jackson looked puzzled. She unwrapped the bag and pulled out a green velvet case.

"It's your pen," Taylor said. "Your real one. I got it back."

"You kidding me? How'd you do that?" Jackson opened the case and pulled out the pen, holding it gently in her hands. "I know that lady wasn't gonna let you swipe something twice in the same day."

Taylor reached in her pocket and handed her a folded piece of paper.

Jackson opened it, confused. "A receipt? What are you saying? Taylor, are you telling me you *bought* me my mom's pen?"

"Yep. That's exactly what I did. Went back into the store like a regular person, told the lady I'd made up my mind and that I wanted to buy the pen I'd been looking at earlier. Same one. Gave her the money in cash and transacted the deal. Straight up."

"Damn, Taylor. I don't think you've ever bought me anything," Jackson laughed, wrapping her arms around the girl. "Thank you, baby."

"Yeah, well, don't get too excited," Taylor said. "Here." She pulled another package out of her pocket and handed it to Jackson. "I stole you a couple packets of cartridges while she was ringing up the sale. I wouldn't want you to be thinking I'm gonna be making a habit of this buying shit."

the wound closed

unsure whether to bleed or heal (since, for the body, both the letting of blood and the pink gathering of tissue are healing—although there is such a thing as just too much loss), the wound closed in sticky yellow struggle. god sighed.

Blue Sky

Taylor took the roach and sucked in hard, held it long, and let it out slow before handing it back to Jackson. The two girls had been lying around most of the afternoon, half sleeping, half getting high, mostly just staying out of the heat. "So how come you never let me hear your story?" she asked.

"What story, baby?" Jackson asked, taking the joint and nuzzling back into her girlfriend's shoulder. "What story you want to hear?"

"You know, the one about how we met. I read you mine but you never let me hear the one that you wrote."

"I'll read it to you, baby," Jackson said. "You know you can read anything I write." Jackson reached over and pulled out her leather journal. "You sure you ready for this?" she asked, smiling.

Taylor grinned and nodded. "Oh yeah."

Jackson sat up a little and began to read out loud:

The white girl seems unaware of how the men are looking at her. That's the first thing I notice about her. She does not engage the eyes of the men. Unless, of course, they are looking for drugs. A friend of Trina's, the white girl comes down to the boulevard to deal. She feeds only the hunger for the drugs; ignores the other hungers, ignores the eyes that want her. The fact that she is not soliciting the men makes them want her even more.

I see everything, even myself—a black girl watching the white girl ignoring the men who are watching her, wanting her. I spit and gently finger my knife. There is something slightly dangerous about this skinny white girl who strides the streets in her heavy boots and possible ignorance, half looking like she owns the territory, half looking like she's just landed from another planet. "Jackson, baby, you just leave that white girl be," my mama warns me. "White girl like that like to get you killed."

Taylor laughed. "Shit. That sounds just like your mom. Always riding my sorry ass about something. You know, I think she hates me worse for being white than being gay."

Jackson smiled. "Nah, she don't hate you. It's just taking a while for you to grow on her, that's all."

"So, you was watching me all that time, too, huh?" Taylor teased, smiling at the thought of Jackson checking her out. "But, damn, then you're watching you watching me, and watching all the motherfuckers, too. What's up with that? Why you gotta write it like you're way up high, looking down on everything?"

"It's called perspective," Jackson said. "The bigger picture. To write well, you've got to be aware of everything."

"Hell," Taylor said, looking back over the story. "I can't hardly keep track of my own damn shit, much less everyone else's."

Jackson laughed. "Yeah, well, you got a lot to keep track of, I'll give you that."

The girls lay back together for a while in silence, enjoying the high. Taylor heard a faint scratching and knew that J. Edger was underneath the camper, digging out a cool place to lie down. She knew that meant that the dog had been let off his chain and she listened for the creaking of hinges and the clanging of the chain-link gates as Jimmy locked up the yard for the night. She figured it had to be close to six and wondered what they should do about food. Maybe she'd sell a lid to one of Jimmy's friends and go get them all burritos. She thought about how much she loved to feel her stomach growl when she had money in her pocket.

"Hey, Taylor," Jackson called softly. "You awake?"

"Uh huh," Taylor answered, pulling her close.

"Girl, you ever been on a plane?"

"A plane?" Taylor asked. "Nah. Oh, you mean like those Lear jets my rich daddy used to fly us in to Paris every summer?"

Jackson ignored her foolishness. "I've been thinking about what we were talking about. I was in a plane once," she said. "When my Nana brought me out here from Detroit. All that morning it had been pouring down rain. Sleet and hail hitting you upside the head so bad you wanted to punch somebody out. Umbrellas were a joke. Cars were sliding off the side of the road all the way to the airport."

Taylor closed her eyes and settled into the story. She briefly wondered what rain and airplanes had to do with their conversation about Jackson's writing, but she was high enough to not care. Besides, she loved the rare moments when Jackson actually told a story out loud instead of always writing in her journal, head buried, unavailable. Jackson didn't talk much, but Taylor learned that if she got her high enough, all that could change real fast.

"So we make it to the airport and get on this big old 727," Jackson continued, "and it takes off right in the middle of the whole damn storm, rumbling down the runway like a motherfuckin' freight train. Then we're up in the air, surrounded by heavy black clouds, hail slamming all up against the windows, lightning everywhere you look, the plane bouncing around all sideways, people screaming and puking in these little bags they so thoughtfully provided. Girl, I was so scared I almost peed my pants.

"'Nana,' I ask her. 'Are we gonna die?'

"And my Nana, she just reaches over, cool as could be, and pats my hand.

"'Well, yes, sugar,' she says. 'Of course we are.'

"So, of course, I almost lose it right then and there and want to book, but where am I gonna run to, right? And so my Nana just smiles and says, 'Honey, we're all a gonna die sooner or later. That's just the way God made us. Now, if what you are asking me is are we going to die right now, on this here plane, well then, baby girl, the answer is no. Of course not. Everything is just fine, sugar. You'll see.'

"And then sure enough, just like she and God had planned it all along, suddenly we bust up through the clouds into this bright blue sky, sun blaring down on the silver wings so you had to squint, all the clouds gone except a sea of white below us, and everything real calm and quiet, like we were floating in space. Then the stewardess straightens her little cap and walks down the aisle with this shiny metal cart that just barely fits, smiling and asking if we'd like a soda and some lunch." Jackson shook her head. "Hot food, too. Already cooked. And we didn't have to pay for it or anything."

"Damn," Taylor said, feeling really hungry now. "Like a fuckin' restaurant in the sky. What did they feed you?"

"I don't know," Jackson said. "I think it was some chicken and gravy and mashed potatoes or something. But that's not the point. Check it out. So, there we are up in the middle of the sky, floating along, me drinking as much root beer as the lady will pour, and my Nana, she takes my hand and points out the window. All I see is blue, no birds, no clouds, nothin'.

"'Sugar,' she tells me. 'I want you to always remember this.'

"'Remember what?' I have to ask, feeling like a knucklehead, but knowing it's not the root beer or the puke bags I'm supposed to be remembering.

"And Nana just keeps pointing out the window. 'All of this,' she says. 'This vast blue sky that goes on forever, even when you can't see that it does. Remember that, baby. Most people think they the clouds, sugar, but you, you are the sky. Now you promise me you won't never forget that.'"

Taylor raised her head and looked over at Jackson. "So, you're the sky, huh?" she grinned, cocking an eyebrow. "You been holding out on me. Damn, girl, and I thought your mama was a trip. Your grandma, she's a fuckin' stoner. They must have had them some kickass reefer back then, that's all I got to say."

"Quit foolin'," Jackson said. "This is serious. I think about this shit all the time, trying to figure out what she was trying to tell me. It's like what I was trying to say about my story. Perspective. My mama says it's all about what you identify with in this world." She nudged Taylor. "How about you?" she asked. "You think you're more like the clouds or the sky?"

"I think you're fuckin' loaded," Taylor laughed. "That's what I think."

Jackson sighed. "Yeah, girl, I'm high, and yeah, I do like your new herb, okay. But I'm serious. If you had to say one, what would you say? You think you'd be the clouds or the sky?"

Taylor looked out the camper window at the thick brown smog that had hung for weeks over the L.A. basin. She wondered how far up into the sky it went, if you could get on a plane and fly right up through it, up into that bright blue sky Jackson's Nana loved so much. She thought about David, the crippled boy next door beat to death by his mom. What was he, she wondered. Was he the sky? She thought about the nights she spent out in the mattress boxes before she hooked up with Jackson, how the cardboard would get all soggy in the rain and collapse in on her as she slept, how she hated the clammy feel of it as she peeled it off. She thought about J. Edgar, chained up all day in the hot, dusty wrecking yard. She thought about their friend Jo-Jo, murdered by some punk-ass john who beat her brains in and then set the place on fire, killing them both.

"Hell, I don't know," she finally said. "When I'm good and loaded, maybe I'm the fuckin' sky. When I'm pissed, then yeah, maybe I'm kinda like the stormy rainclouds and lightning. Coming down hard that time I got strung so bad on Jo-Jo's smack, that's for sure what it's like to be the smog. Rest of the time, for real, I don't think we're either one. I think we're all just the little pieces of shit down here on the ground that get rained on all the time."

Jackson moved her hand up, laying it on Taylor's heart. "Ah, girl," she said softly. "I feel you. Yeah. I don't know. I just can't stop thinking about that sky, that's all. What my Nana was trying to tell me. Like there's something more than all this shit we gotta deal."

"Maybe that just makes it worse," Taylor said, staring back out the window. "I mean, so what if there's a fucking crystal blue sky up there, way above this smog. What the fuck good does that do us anyway if we still got to breathe this shit every day? Like in my story, when that joker clocked me in the alley that day we met, where was the fucking sky then?"

"I don't know, girl," Jackson sighed. "It's more like it's about perspective, I think. Like how my mama always says we are so much more than what was done to us."

Taylor felt her heart catch on something, and then a small rush of anger. "Well," she said, sitting up. "I know what I need. I'm gonna roll me up another bit of perspective right now, with a little blue sky hash thrown in. You all are just too fuckin' deep for me, that's all I gotta say." She reached over for her stash and started rolling the joint, crumbling in little pieces of hash. "I mean, what about Jo-Jo?" she asked. "What's your mama gotta say about Jo-Jo? Is Jo-Jo more than what was done to her? Yeah, she's fuckin' sky, all right. She's fuckin' dead."

Taylor ran her tongue along the seam, twisted the ends, and then handed Jackson the joint. She held the match as Jackson took a long hit and then passed it back.

"I just saw her last week," Jackson said. "Two days before that psycho whacked her. She was looking good, trying to get clean, said she was thinking about getting out."

"Yeah, she got out, all right," Taylor said. She thought about their friend with the soft voice and loud laugh, always flirting with the gay girls, always there to help anyone who was hurting. Taylor fingered the long, jagged scar running down her right bicep. "You remember that time I got cut up so bad and she sewed up my arm?"

Jackson laughed. "Yeah, she was a regular fuckin' Dr. Kildare, carrying around that little sewing kit in her stupid ass candy apple plastic purse, stitching us all up. She taught you pretty good, too."

"Yeah, the best home ec teacher I never had," Taylor said. She looked at the scars on her hands, easily picking out the ones she had sewn up herself. She remembered Jo-Jo leaning over her with such tenderness and attention, holding her rough, bleeding hand in her two clean, manicured ones, always with the bright pink nail polish, tossing whiskey on the cuts like they did in the movies and showing Taylor how to make the small, tight stitches to properly close up a wound. Even when she was strung on smack and about to nod off, Jo-Jo was a perfectionist, making tiny clean sutures and finishing off the ends with a perfectly tied knot. "Remember how she'd always say how she was gonna be a nurse someday and work at a fancy hospital?" Taylor asked.

Jackson shook her head. "Yeah. Man, that's really messed up what happened to her."

The girls smoked the joint down, clipped it, then finished the roach and settled into a mellow, hash-tinged high. Taylor wished they had some music and thought about the portable stereos she's seen down at Montgomery Wards. They were pretty close to the door, she had noticed. Easy enough to steal. They wouldn't be able to play it during the day of course, when the yard was open, but at night, if they kept it real low, it might work out.

"You know what, Taylor?" Jackson said, again breaking the silence. "You know what we gotta do?"

"Damn," Taylor said. "That mind just don't quit, does it?" She stretched out a bit, enjoying the pull of her muscles and the feel of Jackson lying alongside her. "What, baby? What we gotta do?"

"We gotta write Jo-Jo's story," Jackson said.

"How we gonna do that?" Taylor asked. "We don't even really know what happened in there."

Jackson sat up, excited. "No, think about it, girl. Who else is gonna say shit about what happened?"

"Probably nobody, because probably nobody else even gives a shit." Taylor said.

"That's exactly my point," Jackson said. "People die out here all the time and nobody even knows or cares. Come on. Girl was straight and tweaked as hell but she was our girl. We owe it to her, baby. Just think about it. We may not know shit, but we know more about what happened to Jo-Jo than anyone else in this world. Maybe we weren't in that room, but we've been in plenty just like it. Shit, girl. You know what it's like to go upstairs or get into a car when your gut says, 'Uh-uh, fool, don't do it.' You know what it's like to be hurting or stupid enough to do it anyway. And we sure as hell know what it's like to have a psycho trick flip on us. I'm serious about this, Taylor. We know what we need to know. The rest is just details."

Jo-Jo rested at the top of the landing, eyes half closed, fingering a new run in her stockings while the boy fumbled with his keys. Six blocks and six flights of stairs behind her, she knew she'd made a serious mistake the moment she hid her accent, said, "You lookin' for a date, hon?" and agreed to fuck this first-time Johnny.

Jo-Jo's Story

Jo-Jo rested at the top of the landing, eyes half closed, fingering a new run in her stockings while the boy fumbled with his keys. Six blocks and six flights of stairs behind her, she knew she'd made a serious mistake the moment she hid her accent, said "You lookin' for a date, hon?" and agreed to fuck this first-time Johnny. She hardly ever had Asian tricks. They usually went for the white girls around the corner while she got the Anglo businessmen and ex-servicemen looking for something "exotic." Fair-skinned, tonight she was trying to pass for white so she didn't have to deal with their shit, but that hadn't stopped her last trick—the beefy white Texan in the El Dorado—from calling out, "Oh, my little China doll" over and over in a slobbered drawl as he grabbed her hair and pumped his spongy white cock into her mouth, taking forever to come. Jo-Jo felt like spitting up the memory, but swallowed instead, popped another piece of cinnamon gum into her mouth, fingered the cash she'd gotten for blowing the Texan, and walked into the room.

She wanted this over quick. Her feet were killing her; she hadn't eaten or slept since the day before, and she was starting to jones real bad for a fix. She took off her clothes, tucked the money into the side lining of her bag, pulled out a rubber, and glared at the boy still standing stupid and fully dressed. Damn, I don't have time for this shit, she thought, starting to sweat and shake. *You fuckin' bitch, I'll kill you.* The neighbors' voices tore through the walls. *Get out motherfucker before I call the cops.* The Texan drawled in her brain, *Oh, my little China doll, oh, my little China doll.* Her head was exploding. Come on China boy, just fuck me so I can get out of here. She'd seen it before. Asian guys who couldn't get it up except for white meat. Asian guys who couldn't decide whether to beat or fuck the half white in or out of her. The room started to spin. The kid was muttering something about wanting his money back. He "doesn't feel like it" anymore. Christ, give me a break. *Oh, my little China doll...Come here, ya fuckin' cunt...Can I have my money back.... My little China doll...Ya wanna fuck with me, bitch...China doll... China doll...*

"Shut up, you stupid chink! Just shut up and fuck me so I can get out of here." Jo-Jo reached for her clothes. The boy was still talking, louder and louder, whining like a Texan. He grabbed for her bag. "Cut the shit, motherfucker," she warned. The fool thought this was about money. All she wanted was to get out of there, shoot up, and sleep. The gun. She needed somehow to get the gun out of her bag. Quick, she made her move. He slammed her back onto the bed, her fingernails tearing at his eyes. She went for the bag again. She saw him reach for the phone. "Who's the fool think he's gonna call?" she laughed. Then the receiver crashed against her skull. The white light exploding through her head was a relief, the pain clean and clear. *Don't ever mess with a john who can't get it up,* someone was saying, *they can't tell the difference between shame and rage.* By the second blow, she had left her body, blinking into the scene below. She watched the boy continue to flail in slow motion long after she was dead—plastic, batteries, blood, and sweat all raining to the floor.

Free from the brutality of a body, Jo-Jo watched in wonder as the boy began to pump away into the corpse. After he came, he held the empty body's hand for a long time and she almost wept at the loneliness of the brutal child below. Curious, she watched as he set fire to the corpse, the flames moving softly across the room to engulf him as well. His eyes looked calm. For the first time Jo-Jo wondered where she was. Is this death? She thought of her little brother Peewee—fully Chinese, most perfect number one son. How would he touch a woman when he came of age? She thought of the nine hundred dollars burning in her bag and wondered how he and her mom would get by without the money she sent them every month. She thought of her father—the white ghost vet who raped her mother, thinking she was Vietnamese, planting his pale seed just before she brought the kitchen knife down into his back. She thought of her stepfather—the man who married her mother "anyway," hating the soiled girl child. She thought of the calm-eyed boy burning below. Would she see them again in death? She thought of resting against her mother's breast, lilac scented and damp. She thought of a god she long ago stopped believing in. She thought she heard someone say, *I come back roun' fo you, okay?* And then she thought no more.

smoke

tender lungs, sweet pink branches laced with grief's sticky tar. sucking misery. backhand, secondhand smoke; death's breath everywhere the young girl turns. surrounded by smoke. smoke in the womb. smoke in the ward. smoke in the crib. smoke in the everyday kitchen, bedroom, bathroom, living room battles. mom smoking pall mall unfiltered, mom's boyfriend his benson & hedges. grandma loves her winstons. uncle won't smoke anything but camels. mario wraps packs of marlboros up tight into the sleeve of his bright white t-shirt, tucked smooth into his fresh-pressed jeans like a james dean wannabe. the girls smoke, the pros smoke, the pimps smoke, the johns smoke, the pigs smoke, the factories smoke. everyone is smoking, lighting up sorrow. l.a. is burning and the trees, tender and valiant as children, trapped in concrete circles surrounded by a smog-filled sky, browner than the earth, the trees are growing tired.

the girl does not smoke, but still she cannot breathe. surrounded. four adults one child in a car, windows up, breaking down, chain smoking. trapped. smoke at the liquor store, the grocery store, the laundromat; smoke in every public and private space. the girl watches the cigarette burn low, dangling from her mom's drunken hand, ready to catch the ash, or her mother. whichever falls first.

trapped, quiet, barely breathing, the girl watches her uncle across the table, past the meatloaf, mashed potatoes, limp green bean casserole. smoking. he leans back in his chair, takes a long, slow draw, hollywood style, watching her as he exhales. her older cousin shifts, says, "may i please be excused?" gets up to clear the dishes. the uncle's gaze stays on the younger girl and she knows she will be next.

tender lungs, sweet pink branches laced with sticky tar; death's stale breath everywhere she turns. surrounded by smoke, the girl hungers for air, dreams of the sky, longs for sweet rough bark, just one pine-cleansed breath. breaking free, she climbs out of smoky rooms, jumps to the street below, takes in giant gulps of grey-brown l.a. air. smog so thick the flies don't even bother coming 'round. level nine alert. warning! stay inside! curtail all physical activity! p.e. classes cancelled. sports events cancelled.

but never do they cancel the smoke, the exhaustion. never do they cancel the belt, the bottle, the pigs, the perps, the stinking sweaty sheets, all the things a child has to run from each and every grey and sticky day.

Just Another Way to Bleed

Lisa said her mother slapped her when she first got her period.

"No shit?" Trina asked. "Did ya slug her?"

Lisa laughed. "Nah, it wasn't like that. She was all happy and sappy and teary-eyed. Said now I was a *woman*, like that was some sort of good thing to be."

"I was eleven," Jackson said. "Never had anything hurt so bad. Thought my insides were going to rip apart. My mama handed me a brand-new belt and a big ol' pad, then got me a hot water bottle to hold up against my belly."

"Yeah, my mom used to make me wear one of those fat pads, too," Francine laughed. "Said only nasty white girls used tampons. Said I better not be puttin' *anything* up *my* cootchie snatcher." Francine took a long hit on the joint, held it, then exhaled slow, shaking her head. "Like her piece-of-shit boyfriend hadn't already been messing up inside me every night she worked that damn graveyard shift."

Taylor didn't say anything. She thought about the pool of blood her friend Edeena left on the seat in their sixth-grade homeroom when she started her period. She thought about how everyone laughed at her, laughed at Edeena, ruthless king of the tetherball court, the most feared girl on the playground, tougher even than Taylor. She thought about how the P.E. teachers wouldn't let Edeena play sports when she was on her period, and the look on the warrior girl's face as she sat on the bench, slumped and shamed.

Taylor thought about when she started her own period a year later, how she'd hid it from everyone as long as she could, making pads out of the sixteen-pack crew socks stolen from JCPenney's, each one stuffed with rags or paper towels. She thought about Ryan, the boy next door who got beaten so bad by his mom, how the kids would sneak into the locked closet afterwards and tend to his wounds. She thought about how many years she'd been hiding his bloody rags, washing them when she could, dumping or burying them when she couldn't. She thought about how her blood was sometimes brown and clotted, how Ryan's was always fresh red and flowing. She thought about that desperate morning when Ryan's brothers had discovered their mom's tampons and maxi pads, scrambling through the bathroom cupboard for something to help the bleeding boy, crying in the closet. Mike, the oldest, said to "put that shit back," but Taylor marveled at how much blood a maxi pad could soak up, how quick a tampon strapped tight up against a wound could stop the bleeding like nothing else. Quickly, she put two and two together and from then on just stole twelve-pack Tampax slenders, forever leaving the awkward pad-between-the-legs waddle behind, again running wild through the streets, slipping a box to Edeena, grinning as the two skinny girls once more dominated the playground, rightfully owned the ball fields and basketball courts.

Trina said her pimp back in El Paso used to make his girls share the same sponge when he wanted to break them down.

Lisa said hers used to tweak her birth control pills so she'd go longer without a period. "Man, that shit messed me up," she said. "I wouldn't bleed for months and then suddenly start hemorrhaging out like a motherfucker."

"Fuckin' pimps," Francine said. "Who needs 'em! That's why we're renegades!"

"Damn straight," Trina said. "You got that shit right."

And they all hollered and cheered and high-fived each other, laughing. But inside, they all knew. It was just a matter of time before some asshole would take charge of their corner.

Taylor didn't say anything. She thought about the johns who didn't want to fuck a girl on the rag, but how mostly they were clueless. She thought about the blowjobs, hand jobs, sponges, distractions, all the tricks the girls had to just keep on working through. She thought about the jerk in the grey Pontiac, the guy who only wanted to fuck girls who were bleeding, the creep who loved the blood and who, after he was done, wanted you to spank him and tell him what a bad boy he had been. Taylor felt the bile rise up in her throat. *How the fuck do you ever get used to this shit,* she wondered.

"I used to love getting my period when I was a kid," Trina said. "For one, it meant I wasn't pregnant. And, two, it meant I had me a full week, ten days if I was lucky, when that useless clown of a wannabe, cover my closeted lezzie ass boyfriend, didn't want to have sex."

Lisa laughed. "I remember how we used to fake our periods to get out of P.E.," she said. "Strap on a rag and those blond Nazi coaches had to let you sit out."

"Yeah, I used to sometimes fake my cramps," Jackson said. "Pretend they were hurtin' me worse than they were and my mama would let me stay home from school, tuck me all up in a warm, cozy bed, bring me that hot water bottle and a cup of chamomile tea."

She turned to Taylor. "Hey girl," she said, reaching for her hand. "You're awful quiet, today. Whatchu got to say about all this?"

Taylor looked away. "Guess I ain't got nothing to say," she said. "Guess I just don't see what the big fuckin' deal is anyway. All this talk about periods, cramps and shit. You ask me, it all ain't nothin' more than just another goddamn way to bleed in this world."

fear is the hole

fear is not made of any fabric i know how to touch. i can't just find a thread and follow it to its source. run my fingers along rough yarn leading one way to the tightly woven pattern now unraveling in my hands, nor the other way toward the soft grey ball gathering into itself and say, yes, this is it, this is my fear. this is where my fear has come. this is where my fear will lead. because, even as i sit both weaving and unraveling the meaning of my life, i know, fear is not the fabric, fear is the hole. fear is the hole in the sweater. the tear in the cloth. the missing sleeve. and though there is terror at the edges, frayed and gaping into the hole. and though there is pain in the worn, severed pieces, snipped and fallen to the floor, still, fear is not the fabric. fear is in the holes. fear is what gets left in the vacuum of a young girl's chest when faith is sucked and smothered, spit out in the toilet bowl. fear is the chasm of waiting. fear is the fall. fear is the hole left in the night sky when all the screams have stopped.

tracks

As soon as Taylor crossed the railroad tracks, she knew something was wrong. Throat tight, she broke into a jog, cresting up out of the last dusty ravine. Behind her, the August sun was setting, turning the smog crimson. Below, inside the wrecking yard she called home, red lights and police radios. The torn section of chain-link fencing that was the girls' private entrance gaped open, unsecured.

She heard a soft voice call her name and turned to see Jackson, sitting crouched up against a boulder, waiting.

"What the fuck happened?" she asked, looking around. "What the fuck is all this?"

Jackson got up and walked over to her. "It's over, baby. The pigs got Jimmy. We gotta get out of here."

"What do you mean the pigs got Jimmy?" Taylor asked, confused. "Jimmy's clean."

Jackson glared at her, disgusted. "Girl, you've been around enough to know that doesn't mean shit. Of course Jimmy's clean. Mama says a successful black man is the biggest threat of all, way more dangerous than the thugs and the junkies. You see how it is. Mama says they take the good brothers down, give the rest guns and the white man's drugs, and sit back and watch the fun." She spit on the ground and slowly kicked dry dirt over it with her boot. "Anyway, it doesn't matter. They got Jimmy, the place is crawling with pigs, and we can't go back."

Taylor felt like she was going to be sick. She thought of Jimmy, letting them stay for free in the yard, teaching her how to strip down a car for parts. She thought about how last week he let her rig up the cherry picker and pull an engine out of a wrecked Chevy all by herself. She thought about how happy he was working at the new free breakfast program the Panthers had set up down at the church. Rage rose like bile in her throat as she thought about him in the hands of the police. She wished she could reach over to Jackson, pull her in close, hold her tight up against her heart, but she knew there was no way her lover would let herself be touched right now. "Well," she said. "Guess we gotta go get our shit out of the fuckin' camper, and then find a place to stay tonight."

Jackson pointed to the small pile she had gathered by the boulder. "I got our stash, all my journals and some clothes, and grabbed what I could of yours."

Taylor picked up the pillowcase, bulky, heavier than she expected. Reaching inside, she rummaged through the books and dirty clothes, felt some plastic crinkling and pulled out the pack of new boxer briefs Jackson had just bought her. She laughed. "What the fuck. Shit's going down and you grab my fuckin' skivvies?"

Jackson smiled. "Yeah. It's like that thing where they say your house is on fire and you've only got sixty seconds to get out everything that matters. So, yeah, I grabbed your dope, books, and boxers." She looked suddenly shy, and sad. "Besides," she said. "You didn't really have much to grab."

"It's cool," Taylor said, risking a grin. "I'm glad you grabbed my shorts. So, where do you want to stay tonight? I don't really want to hit the boxes. We could try Randi, see if he's working tonight, maybe get us a car. Or see if we could crash in Trina's room, except we'd probably have to wait until three or four in the morning, whenever they're done tricking."

"Taylor," Jackson interrupted softly, touching her cheek. "I'm not going with you."

"What do you mean?" Taylor asked. "What are you saying? You said we couldn't stay here anymore. That's pretty obvious. So, we gotta find another place to crash."

"I mean I gotta really get out of here. Here," she gestured. "This whole fuckin' place. L.A. The strip. Tricking. The hustle. The whole damn thing. I'm not like you. I just can't take it anymore."

Taylor grabbed her arm, turning the girl toward her. "What the fuck is that supposed to mean? Shit. Can't none of us take it. You just do it anyway. You taught me that. Come on. I'll figure something out for us. We'll be okay."

Jackson leaned back into her lover's arms. "Nah, baby. I gotta get out of here. I've been sitting up on this rock waiting for you, thinking shit through. I can't do it anymore. I just gotta leave this place." Anticipating Taylor's response, she added, "Alone."

Taylor held on, forcing herself to breathe. "So where you gonna go?"

"I've got an auntie down in San Diego, once told me I could live with her if I cleaned up and went to school. Said there's a community college I could get into and she'd help me out. Mama says I should do it and I'm thinking maybe she's right."

Taylor turned and started walking down the trail to the torn fence.

"Taylor," Jackson called out. "Where are you going? You can't go back in there."

Taylor kept walking. "I'm going in to get J. Edgar," she said. "Jimmy's gone. You're gone. Somebody's got to take care of the damn dog."

"Taylor, stop!" Jackson ran to catch up. "Listen to me—you can't go in there. There's pigs everywhere."

"I don't care about the fuckin' pigs," Taylor said. "I'm going to get J. Edgar."

"Goddamnit, Taylor. Stop." Jackson grabbed her arm. "Will you just fucking stop and listen to me? You can't go back in and get J. Edgar because J. Edgar is dead."

Taylor stopped and turned back, her voice hard and low. "What do you mean? What are you saying?"

"I'm saying that J. Edgar is dead. The pigs shot him." Jackson started to cry. "He was trying to protect Jimmy and the fuckin' cops just fuckin' shot him. He's dead, girl. I saw it all."

Taylor spun back around, glaring down at the yard where the police cars flashed red blue, red blue, and bright white strobes lit up the back shed Jimmy had made home. Hot rage punched through her chest and she saw herself flying down the hill like a dust devil tornado, crashing through the cyclone fence, kicking out car windows, slugging cops. *Just shoot me, you motherfuckin' pigs! Why you gotta shoot J. Edgar? Come on, you piece of shit coward-ass punks. Just fuckin' shoot me!*

But up on the hill there was nothing to slug, no sheetrock to ram her fist through, no tail lights to kick in, no drunken johns to take down. Taylor heard Jackson softly crying behind her, heard the crackle of police radios in the yard below and the whir of a police helicopter approaching from the south. When she saw the chopper crest the ridge, Taylor turned back to Jackson. "Come on," she said. "Let's get outta here."

The two girls gathered up their bundles and walked the two miles to the Greyhound station in silence. As they said goodbye, Jackson asked softly, "So what are you gonna do now, baby?"

"I'm gonna find me a fuckin' place to sleep, that's what," Taylor answered, avoiding her eyes.

"No, girl, I'm serious. I mean, what you gonna do with your life?"

"My life?" Taylor laughed. "What the fuck is that supposed to mean? My life. What am I going to do with my life? Shit. I thought I was already doing it."

Taylor walked away, leaving Jackson to catch the next dog going south. She crossed Cahuenga and walked down past Hollywood Boulevard, barely stopping for the lights, glaring at anyone who honked, daring them to get out of their cars and just try and start something with her. She walked past the upholstery shops and taquerias, past the KFCs and burger stands, past the peep shows on Sunset, walked until she found Tyrone, standing on his corner, leaning back against the wall.

"Hey," he nodded to her, smiling. "How's my favorite chipper? You looking kind of hungry tonight, girl. Want me to cook somethin' up for you? I got an extra kit right around the corner, just in case you aren't carrying yours in your Huck Finn wannabe pillowcase. No charge. It's on the house."

Taylor felt her veins jump in anticipation, but just said, "Fuck you. Like I'm gonna use your skanky works. Nah," she said. "Just give me a couple of nickel bags. You got something good enough to blow?"

She made the buy and continued walking, taking Santa Monica down to Wilshire, walking for miles as the cars turned into Porsches and Bentleys and the trash stayed mostly in the cans. She stopped in front of the Sheraton, stashing her gear in the bushes across the street and watching the valet stand until she saw what she was looking for. She crossed over and caught Randi coming back from parking a shiny new black Mercedes.

"Hey, man," she called out. "You got any accommodations tonight?"

"Girl!" His hug lifted her off the ground. "It's good to see you! What you doing in this part of town?"

She pulled away, handed him one of her nickel bags. "Just need a place to crash for the night. Can you help me out?"

He took the packet and looked around. "No problem," he said, handing her the keys to the Mercedes. "I've got just the thing. They're in for the night. Stay low, sleep tight, and come see me in the morning. I'll try and get you into the staff locker room and get you cleaned up a bit."

Taylor went back to get her gear, checked out the surroundings, then climbed into the back of the Mercedes. She locked the doors and let out a sigh, grateful for the dark, tinted windows. Tomorrow, she knew, everything would be just as fucked up, but tonight, just for a while, she would rest. She breathed in the wonderful new car smell, mixed with a faint lingering scent of a woman's expensive perfume. She imagined Jackson with her, breathing deep, saying, "Girl, can't you just *smell* that money!" Taking out her remaining nickel bag, she cut the lines, rolled the bill, and took two quick, deep breaths. Her nostrils burned and she fought the first blast of nausea, then gave in, slumping back into the soft, still-warm, custom leather seats.

PART THREE

The Work

the daughter's job

It is the daughter's job to keep her mother alive. Each night from her small bed the girl guides her mother home safe from the outside world. She sees her mother leave the bar and get in the car. No men follow her, stumbling, drunk; no one puts their hands on her. No police bother her. The mother starts the engine and pulls slowly out into the street. Careful, she drives up the freeway onramp, staying between the lines, changing lanes safely, with her turn signal on so the police won't stop her, carefully taking the right exit to their house, making two left turns, one right, another left. Then she pulls up into the driveway and turns off the ignition.

Once she gets home, of course, the girl lives in terror of what her mother might do, for she is what they call a mean drunk. Still, each night, the girl carefully and intently brings her mother safely home. One night the girl falls asleep before the time when her mother usually leaves the bar and her grandma wakes her in the early morning to take her to a neighbor's house, telling her that her mother has been in a car crash and is in the hospital. The mother lives—a few cracked ribs, some ugly bruises. The girl never falls asleep again without first bringing her mother home.

The girl gives up her body to keep her mother alive. Yields, as children have done for centuries, to the inexorable parental pull which feeds on a child's spirit, body, emotional being. The child's desire to please. The child's desire to serve. No membranes to protect these desires from the parent's hunger. Nights when the mother is calm, drunk but not fighting mad, she lies on top of the daughter, mumbling the name of a man the daughter does not know. Following nature's law, the girl submits, as always, to the weight of the mother, lies still, catches breath when she can, leaves her body when she cannot. Silent, she endures the musky woman scent sometimes mixed with the vomit-stenched strands of hair crossing her face. The mother moans. The girl suckles. There is no milk. Everything female is hungry and there is no sustenance to be found.

Some winters when times are tough and there is too much anger and not enough food, the girl is sent to live with her aunt and uncle across the valley. Nights, the aunt tucks the girl child into bed, gently covering her with a soft worn quilt of muted colors and familiar patterns. Nights, the uncle removes the quilt and, as always, the girl child submits to the larger force, the pull of a desire she cannot understand but can only serve, as centuries of girls have done before her. She makes her mouth into the big O shape her uncle requests, hides her teeth beneath her lips as he has taught her, and takes his thick snake swollen into her throat. Sometimes the corners of her mouth tear. She fights to not throw up whatever food is in her belly. Sometimes she has to breathe through her spine for her mouth can find no air. Sometimes he makes her swallow his milky cum, saying yes, lap it up like a good girl, lap it all up now. It is the daughter's job to feed the uncle. Again, the girl goes to bed hungry.

When the girl begins to bleed, she leaves her mother and uncle's homes and goes to live on the streets of the city. She joins packs of other wild girls, fighting to the death, eating from the dumpsters, charging for the sex that is being taken from them anyway. Sometimes they keep the money. Always they share with the younger girls. Sometimes the older boys steal it from them. Sometimes the boys with guns try to capture the wild girls and pimp them out for all the money. Sometimes the police trap them and then all business has to stop while the girls service the police, one by one by one by one, in exchange for protection.

The girl ranges from pack to pack, hungry, refusing to be owned, refusing to die. It is the daughter's job to keep herself alive. She learns how to use a knife. She learns to steal and cut without a backward glance. She learns all the things a white man wants from a girl. For all her customers are white men from the owning class. Her uncle has taught her well. So the girl ranges hungry, selling the tricks of her body but refusing to be owned.

And one night she curls on the floorboard of a 1969 Cadillac Seville, servicing the beefy Texan, thinking of the food she will buy with the fifty dollars she's earned for blowing him without a rubber, great breasts of fried chicken, mashed potatoes with gravy, lemon meringue or chocolate cream pie. And then the man makes a mistake and speaks. Grabbing the girl's head, he says, "Oh god girl, yes, suck me hard, suck me like my little baby girl sucks me." And the girl's head pulls back as she spits out his cock. And she bares her teeth and snarls. And she feels her right hand reach down into her right black boot, pulling out the thin silver blade. Pressing it hard against the Texan's gut, the girl is hungry for the kill. She wants to cut this white hairball belly so bad she can almost taste it. But who really wants to taste such flesh?

Ultimately, the girl does not kill because she refuses to be owned, even by death. Hunger is the only master she allows and even he will not have her tonight. She draws a thin red line through the belly hairs just above the spongy, flaccid cock. A little blood runs onto the slick leather seats. The girl forces the Texan out of the car, taking his wallet, keeping his keys. She keeps his shoes, his pants and his sports jacket, leaves him standing barefoot and bleeding on the corner of La Cienega Blvd. She starts the car and slowly pulls out into the street. She drives up the freeway onramp, staying between the lines, changing lanes safely, with her turn signal on so the police won't stop her. She knows she will have to sell the credit cards soon while they are still fresh, before they spoil. She calculates the time, wondering if the street jackals will find the Texan before he finds a telephone that works. She knows that soon she will have to dump the car, sell it cheap or send it over the cliffs of Malibu into the silver sea. She knows that soon she will be back on the streets. But for now, she drives. It is the daughter's job to keep herself alive.

Pigs and Donuts

"Hey, baby, bring us some more coffee, will ya?"

I spit in their coffee. And carry it to their table, talking to my body like it was somebody else: "Now, don't you mess me up here, we can't show no fear, okay. We just go in and out real smooth, no shaking, no tripping, no spilling. We just gonna set this shit down on the table real calm and professional like we're some college girl and then we gonna get back behind the counter." When I get my feet all talked into not stumbling and my hands convinced they gonna set the coffee down *on the table* and not in the faces or crotches of these motherfucking pigs I got to wait on, then I move. But it's all gotta happen real fast, these jokers don't like to wait. I tried for a while to talk my mouth into smiling like a straight girl but it wasn't gonna happen so I let it slide. It wasn't ever my mouth they looked at anyway.

So, here I am working graveyard shift at Winchell's Donut House on Ventura Boulevard. Keeps me warm and dry at night, lets me hustle up easy daytime money. I didn't last too long on the night streets after Jackson left. It was okay; I mean, the money was easy and it felt good to be setting the price and terms for something that was gonna get taken from me anyway. And me and the other girls, we was tight. Got us formed all together like a pack of wild dogs (they called 'em "worker collectives" in the books I read, but I knew what they meant), and for a while nobody messed with us. Some john dick or harry try and pull something too kinky or not pay you or some shit and the other girls would be on his ass like white on rice. For some of 'em that was their favorite part of the trade. Yeah, we had some good times. Those girls never did stop trying to get me into a dress, but, like my smile at the donut store, it just wasn't gonna happen. And they still called me Mahatma and made fun of my books and I still called them queens and told 'em they'd never look as pretty as the boys round the corner in West Hollywood. We was tight. But it all got fucked up. For one thing, everywhere I looked I saw Jackson, leaning up against the side ally, looking all fly, pointing down with a grin at the boot where she kept her damn knife, breaking my heart into ten thousand pieces each and every fuckin' time.

For another, the shiny boys who dealt and carried wanted a piece of the action. They didn't think no females should be making that kind of money without givin' it to Poppa, so we had some problems. Also, we couldn't do nothing about the police. Seemed like no matter how many we sucked and fucked, they just kept coming back 'round. They fucking multiplied like bunnies. They must have had the whole damn police force working vice and narcotics so they could get laid and stoned and then make some money from the payoffs and the stash they stole on busts.

But, hey, check it out. Here I am again surrounded by the motherfuckers. Come to find out my boss has a deal with the police that if they come around his store a lot for "protection," he (which means I) will give them free coffee and donuts. The truth is I would much rather be robbed than protected, in fact I was working the last two times this store went down and it was cool. These brothers came in with weapons and all and I didn't even have to tell my body nothin'. My feet stayed calm, my hands were steady, and damn if my mouth wasn't grinning wide and pretty as I asked them if they'd like some jelly donuts to go with the cash drawer I was emptying for them.

But that was just twice. The rest of the time, night after night I have to serve these pigs coffee and listen to them go off braggin' about the niggers beaners spics and faggots whose heads they've cracked and the hippies whores and dykes they've raped and messed up good. Like now they're talkin' right in front of me like I don't even exist except to bring them more donuts, which I guess is good since I belong to a few of the categories they like to fuck with and my friends belong to the rest. But it freaks me out to be so invisible, even though it saves my ass. It's like I'm in some sort of Nazi spy movie and it's only the whiteness of my skin and this thin white polyester donut uniform that keeps them from recognizing me as the enemy and killing me, too.

And I can't help but wonder if they're the same ones that took Jimmy away. The same motherfuckin' ones that shot J. Edgar. I keep thinking I ought to be doing something more than spitting in their coffee. My hands say, just give us a gun and we promise you we will not shake or tremble, and in my mind I see their bodies sprawled out all over the floors I have to scrub each night. But the truth is I just stay invisible and try and keep from showing my fear. It's all I can do to not throw up or piss on myself and I cannot stop the sweat from running down my back and sides as I sweep the floors, wipe the counters, load the glazes, and lay out the chocolate sprinkles in seven crooked rows.

Train Ride

"Okay, girl. You gotta get to runnin'. Now! We'll take care of the bulls; you just make sure you get a good grip on that number three piggyback coming up here. Then you fly on up top of that thing and lie flat till you're out of town. And don't you go swinging your legs around either or you'll wind up like Eddie here, boppin' around on two stumps."

The first thing you need to know about riding a freight train is to listen to the old guys out in the yard. You may think you're pretty fly and that you have hopped plenty of trains before, but when the bums take you in and teach you how to properly ride a freight train you will realize you don't know shit.

Sitting in the dusty railroad yard camp, drinking Red Mountain and listening to these guys, you will feel happy. You figure since you're working such a shitty job at Winchell's Donut House, you should get some real vacations like other folks that work straight jobs. Your boss won't like it but nobody else wants to work that damn night shift and besides he knows you know he knows you ain't no twenty-one years old like you're supposed to be to work graveyard and he don't want no bait trouble coming down. So here you are with your favorite vacation package plan.

Which goes like this: Hitchhike up to Santa Barbara and if something better doesn't happen on the ride, then get off at the Highway One stoplights and walk down to the railroad yards, stopping off for a bottle or two of their best rotgut wine. There you meet up with your friends at the yard for an evening of entertainment, and the next morning hop the grey ghost going north, dropping acid when you first get on so that by the time you're peaking the train will be heading over the gorge bridge and you're lying on the flat piggyback car with no load on it 'cept you and no side rails just a full-on drop off both sides down two hundred feet into the Pacific Ocean. Oh yeah, and the sun is pounding down and there is only the sound of the tracks and everything sparkles. Sometimes you won't even take acid and then you'll have five full hours of peace and quiet where you can just read and there ain't nobody messing with you. Then you get off the train when it slows down outside Pajaro because the bulls are fierce and besides you really don't want to wind up in San Jose. Then you hitchhike toward the coast. If your ride goes north when you hit the ocean, you party in Santa Cruz and maybe shake down the rich hippy kids at the university. If it heads south, then it's Big Sur and back down Highway One and home again.

The hobos will all take real good care of you, treat you like a queen or movie star or something. You'll drink wine with them and they will tell stories by the fire and if somebody's language gets a little rough (like yours isn't, right?), someone will hit him and holler out, "Hey, watch your fucking language, asshole, we got a lady present." They'll make sure you always get the best place to sleep, like if they can unlock a station wagon at the used car lot. Your favorite place will be the empty boxes behind Montgomery Wards. The hobos all like the mattress boxes because they can stretch out, but you'll go for the refrigerator boxes 'cause you can crawl in when it's on its side and then have your friends tilt it upright so you're all curled up inside with four walls covering your back and can't nobody try and get in without you knowing about it first.

This will be your favorite vacation. You may have others, but this one's the best.

Lassie

The first time Taylor's grandma almost came out to California was when she was eight years old and a rich couple rode through town in a fancy carriage and heard her singing in the church choir. They took her daddy aside and told him she was real pretty and mighty talented, and if he'd like they'd take her off his hands and give her a good life. It would have been a good deal for her daddy, since they were dirt-poor Kansas farmers and she provided the least help of all the nine kids, ever since she'd gotten bit by a rattler and almost died. But she was the baby and her daddy was partial to her, snake bit and all, so he told the couple that he was much obliged but where he came from folks took care of their own.

When Taylor was younger and heard the story of her grandma, she used to think that if a rich couple ever drove down her street looking for a kid she'd definitely figure out a way to go with them. She couldn't sing worth shit but she could steal stuff for them and tell stories and take care of their horses. She knew her dad wouldn't mind so long as he made a profit on the deal. He was always hustling something up, like when he talked the doctor into taking her out of her mom a few weeks early on December 30 because he heard he could get an income tax write-off if his kid was born before year end. Then he made side bets with the other expectant dads in the waiting area about which kid was going to get born first, but of course he didn't tell them Taylor was going to be cesarean and he'd seen the doctors' operating schedule. The other dads were pissed, but what could they do? He got their money and the write-off, too.

The next time Taylor's grandma almost came out to California was in the '20s. She'd married a traveling salesman/auctioneer who told her he was on to something big and as soon as he made it out west he'd send for her. But he never did and she just kept on scrubbing toilets and taking in laundry and sewing while her boy worked his ass off all day and studied theater at night. He was going to be a famous actor and then he was going to beat up his daddy for leaving them all the time and making his mama work till her hands bled.

The third time, Taylor's grandma actually got to go to California—her boy won the "Gateway to Hollywood" contest, packed up his mama and little baby sister, and took them all out west. He never did get to be the serious actor he dreamed about, and she scrubbed California toilets and laundry for the next fifteen years. But by the time Taylor was born her uncle had married a Hollywood actress who paid his way until he got to be the super famous star of the *Father of the Year* TV series, and then things were going pretty good for him.

A few times Taylor got to go down to the Universal Studios back lot to watch them film the show. It was always really funny because her uncle hated the kids who played his son and daughter—called the boy a bucktooth little snot and the girl a spoiled princess bitch— and when the cameras weren't on he'd yell at the kids just like he was a real dad. Then they'd start shooting and he'd turn into this stern but loving father that people still talked about.

One time Taylor's mom got her all dressed up, tight shoes and all, to go to an awards ceremony for her eleven-year-old cousin

Kevin, who had won this big citywide contest for an essay he wrote on "Why My Dad Should Be Father of the Year." It was in the news and everything and Taylor's uncle proudly showed the paper to all his friends. Taylor and her mom got seated right up front with her uncle's family, and when the lights went off and her cousin started reading his essay, she almost died because Kevin was telling stories about the television character instead of his own dad and some of the stories were right out of the episodes. Taylor snuck a look at her other cousins, but they looked scared and she couldn't laugh or anything because she could tell her uncle noticed too and he was definitely not amused. His jaw was clenched and the veins were pumping on the side of his forehead, and she knew Kevin was going to see the wrong end of the belt that night.

Taylor thought it was a pretty good joke and possibly worth a licking, but later she found out Kevin wasn't even trying to be funny. She understood it all better when she went to live with her cousins for a while and saw how when her uncle got drunk he didn't get all mean and violent like her mom but instead got real serious and tried to have these heavy talks with the kids, but his words always came out as lines he'd said on the TV show. It made Taylor feel creepy as hell, but apparently it was really comforting for Kevin and he loved it when his daddy talked to him that way. So he meant his essay to be sweet but he got a whupping anyway.

Taylor's grandma was always telling stories about how great her husband was (and never about how he walked out on them all), but she couldn't ever tell them in front of Taylor's uncle because he was still pissed about having to be husband, father, and son before he was eighteen. One time he got a big check for doing a fancy detective movie, and it must have given him ideas because he hired a private detective to track down his daddy. After a while the detective gave him an address in Memphis. When her uncle got there he discovered his daddy living with a woman who claimed him as her husband. Taylor's uncle was going kill him, but his wife called to say his agent had gotten him a good part on *The Lassie Show* and so he came home instead.

Taylor thought it was pretty cool that her uncle got to meet Lassie until he laughed at her and explained there wasn't really a "Lassie" but actually seventeen Lassies that looked almost the same but got used for different things. Turned out there were Lassies for falling down cliffs and Lassies for swimming across rivers—actually lots of swimming Lassies because when they'd reshoot a scene they had to start over with a dry Lassie each time. Then there was the Lassie that barked for Timmy and the one that lifted up his paw and whined. Taylor didn't believe her uncle at first, because for one thing she couldn't trust anything anybody in her family said, and for another, even though she was a pretty tough and savvy kid, she'd really believed Lassie was real and it frightened her to think that maybe the TV people made up a dog that saved kids just like they made up parents that didn't drink or hit.

Her uncle brought back photos of lots of Lassies in cages on a studio truck. That was always a good adult joke—finding something a kid believed in and then showing her how stupid she was for believing it. Taylor didn't get tricked very often, mostly because she didn't talk when adults were around, but that time she did and her uncle told that story for years at her expense.

It was okay, though; Taylor had her share of jokes. Her favorite was actually her mom's boyfriend's joke, but she got to see it once so she claimed it as her own.

Sometimes the family would get all dressed up and go out to fancy movie-star restaurants with her aunt and uncle. Taylor's mom would get to borrow one of her aunt's elegant dresses, and her uncle would give the boyfriend a nice sports jacket and tie. The first part of the joke was that the boyfriend was a vacuum cleaner salesman, but when he dressed up in the uncle's clothes he looked just like the actor Richard Widmark. Later, when he got older, he looked like Gerald Ford, but that's another joke.

The second part of the joke came when they were all sitting down to eat at this fancy-ass restaurant and a group of autograph seekers spotted their table and began to make their way over, all giggly, whispering and pointing. Taylor's uncle puffed up real big and prepared to be the gracious star, but the group went right up to her mom's boyfriend instead and said, "Oh, Mr. Widmark, could we *please* have your autograph. We just love your movies." The boyfriend laughed and joked with them for a while, asking which of "his" films they liked best. When Taylor's mom saw how pissed her brother was getting, she kicked her boyfriend under the table and he kissed the girls' hands and signed their books, "I will always remember this night, best regards, Dick." It was a perfect night, and during all the commotion Taylor got to pocket three of the extra forks they give out at places like that, plus a silver linen napkin and two ashtrays.

Taylor took care of her grandma every day when she got out of school, and they had a pretty good time. Taylor hated cooking meals so some nights she'd fool her grandma and tell her they'd already had dinner—she was pretty forgetful by then—and what they were doing now was making pies for dessert. Grandma would just say, "Oh," and then settle into making the best crust in the world while Taylor made the lemon meringue or double chocolate Jell-O pudding fillings. Then they'd eat pies together and Taylor would get to hear those famous tales.

Grandma loved to tell stories—about rattlesnakes, rich people, and the crazy folk in California—and Taylor loved to listen to her. She sometimes got teased about how when she was little she always used to ask, "Grandma, is that *true*?" Grandma would laugh and say, "Honey, you look around us here in *this* family in *this* town and you tell me something that's *true*, and then I'll tell you about my stories."

When Taylor's grandma died, her mom kind of went off the deep end and Taylor had to move out of the house before someone— usually her—got hurt. Crazy as they were, the streets actually felt safe, predictable by comparison.

Years later, Taylor was living with a high-end sex worker in West Hollywood and working at a place called Eddie's Speakeasy over in Pasadena when she heard that her uncle had died. Eddie had been born male but always felt female. After she transitioned to female she still liked dressing like a man so she kind of looked like a big-breasted dyke in drag. She spoke in a higher-pitched queen's voice but she could throw a guy clear out into the street if someone broke the rules of the "speakeasy." There were rooms in the back for turning regular tricks, but Taylor worked out in front where there were these tacky booths built for johns who wasted the prostitute's time when they wanted to talk rather than fuck. Somebody came up with the idea as a joke, but it took off, and Eddie charged these guys thirty bucks a half hour to sit and talk with a girl—no touching allowed. It was great. Taylor had a job, didn't have to touch the motherfuckers, Eddie made good money, and the women in the back could get down to business. So, that's where she was when her girlfriend called and said she'd read in the paper that Taylor's uncle was dead.

Taylor called her mom, who said she was going to have a special memorial service at her house—no, the others didn't approve, but goddammit he was her brother and the service was going to be at her own goddamn house, and yes, she could use Taylor's help. When Taylor arrived her mom explained there would be newspaper reporters and a lot of important people, so the place had to look really classy. Taylor laughed, looking around at the orange carpet, peeling linoleum, and three-foot-high weeds in the back yard. "Right, Mom. Classy."

She had her mind set, though, so Taylor just went along for the ride and let her mom do her thing, which turned out to be pretty incredible. She was a great cook when she was sober, and the house cleaned up pretty good, and Taylor mowed the weeds down low so they almost looked like grass. Her mom gave her a can of green spray paint to cover over the dirt spots, but the Santa Ana winds picked up and blew wet, green dirt everywhere, so she gave up on that. Then, an hour before people were supposed to arrive, her mom looked up and panicked. "The walls! Classy places are supposed to have pictures on the walls." Taylor told her to forget it but she was on a roll. "No, I know just the thing. Come on!"

She dragged Taylor to the hardware store to buy some one-by-twos and nails and then across the street to JCPenney's, where she'd seen huge beach towels on sale. Rummaging through the pile she found two velour ones and then they tore out of there and back to the house. In ten minutes Taylor's mom had hammered together frames and pulled the towels tightly over them, stapling it all together in the back. Then she stood up on the back of the couch, hammering into the wall, and Taylor handed her the "prints" to hang as high up as she could reach. When someone knocked on the door, she stashed the hammer behind the couch.

Taylor went out back on the "lawn" to smoke a joint and watch people arrive. There were some people from her uncle's church, a lot she didn't know, all her cousins and then, in a surreal parade, the cast of the *Father of the Year* show, all fat and grown up. Darin Saunders, the guy who played the son, was looking pudgy and wannabe suave with a woman in a tight black evening dress, loitering right under the new "prints." Taylor had to admit the pictures looked pretty damn good—they were two abstract silhouettes, global continents all shiny black against a shimmery gold background that actually did tie in nicely with the orange carpet and black couch. Taylor appreciated the joke. She wished her grandma was there to see it, but figured she and her uncle were probably watching the whole show from above. Or below.

She came back inside to find Darin, with tears in his eyes, telling her cousin Kevin how her uncle had been just like a father to him. And Carolyn Chandler, who looked exactly the same and talked just like she had on the show as the "good housewife," had a drink in one hand and Taylor's mom's arm in the other and was telling her how absolutely stunning her two prints were, and where did she possibly find such lovely abstract representations of the world?

Taylor's mom took a long drag on her cigarette. She struck a dramatic pose, paused for effect, then exhaled real slow. "Oh, those old things." She smiled, flicking her hand in the direction of the prints. "They're just a little something I picked up on a trip somewhere. I'm so glad you like them, Carolyn dahling." Taylor wasn't sure which movie star her mom was imitating, but she was riding pretty high, thoroughly enjoying herself.

She glanced over at Taylor, arching her eyebrows and pursing her lips in a familiar *what did I tell you?* look. The girl raised her glass in a mock toast. Then she moseyed over to the makeshift bar, where her uncle's old publicity lady was hustling a former stunt man who said he was Tony Curtis' double in *Some Like It Hot.* It was a pretty good joke because he thought he might get a part out of her, but he didn't know she was just a rich old drunk who didn't have any clout left in Hollywood. The agent thought she might get some hot sex from his still-studly body but Taylor knew that wasn't going to happen because she'd already seen him outside hitting on her two gay friends, whom she'd traded dope to in exchange for providing "valet parking services," which in reality just meant making sure the cars were still there, hubcaps and all, when people wanted to leave.

But the best part of the joke wasn't either of these clowns. It was the gold-sequined pocketbook dangling off the back of the publicity lady's barstool. Taylor had spotted it earlier when the lush interrupted her story of all the women Taylor's uncle had fucked to clasp the girl's head to her damp lilac-scented bosom, rock her around a little, and mutter, "Oh dear, what a loss. What a tremendous loss this must be for you kids. He was such a god. A true icon." The right side of her face was pushed into the gold sequins of the lady's sweaty gown straining against her breasts, but out of her left eye Tayor glanced down and saw the matching gold purse, its clasp slightly open, revealing a gold-plated cigarette case and seriously bulging gold-sequined wallet. Now here it was again, that shimmering pocketbook right in front of her eyes, swinging just below the lady's broad gold-sequined ass, gaping open in a sweet offer Taylor just couldn't refuse.

Screwing the Rich

"C.N., get your hands off that girl. This ain't no lesbo porn movie we're filming here."

I hear the voice as if it's far off down a tunnel in somebody else's dream. A few minutes ago I was so messed up on the Quaaludes and hash they gave us before filming that I was feeling absolutely no pain. In fact, I wasn't feeling much of anything except hot lights and sweaty bodies pushing against the numbness of this body that was about to pass out. We were filming the scene where the hero stud comes to California, meets up with some hippies, they all smoke from a hookah pipe, and then immediately break into a wild orgy. I was trying to stay conscious because otherwise I wouldn't get paid, but I was losing it. Next thing I knew I got like shot through this tunnel of sensation and everything went from being numb and blurry to being bright and intense. And I don't mean the lights. Now I am full-on pressed right up against the body of this woman they seem to be yelling at and I wonder if I am "that girl" they are talking about. All I know is that every cell in my body is suddenly alive; I am inhaling this woman, my face is buried in her neck, and I am feeling pleasure in places in my body I'd forgotten even existed. And check it out. I am feeling pleasure right in the middle of filming a goddamn porn scene. I'm telling you, in Hollywood fact is stranger than fiction. Not only am I feeling pleasure like, honey, someone just turned on the light switch after years of darkness, but it's like my heart got reattached, too. I don't know what the fuck is going on except that I am probably gonna lose a really good job but they are definitely gonna have to tear me away from this woman that is stealing my sorry-ass heart right here and now.

"Cut! Goddammit, C.N. I told you to knock it off. I'm not gonna have any kinky shit in my film. This is not a lesbian movie."

"Oh, but that's exactly what it is," she laughs. "Come on, darlin. I'm taking you home."

I manage to get up, get my clothes on, and watch this woman reach over and put on a cowboy hat left over from the scene where the hero-stud did the Dallas Cowboy cheerleaders. Then she smiles at me and I pass out.

When I wake up I am in fuckin' heaven. That's all I can say. She's still smiling at me, only now I am lying in her bed, in her apartment. In her fancy-ass penthouse apartment. In her bed that looks like it could sleep ten people and you could just sink right down into the softness of pillows all around you and a huge feather pillow underneath you. And it smells so sweet. Man, she can't hardly get me outta that bed. Not that she tries too hard. Turns out she's working the trade, but on some completely different level. She turns like two or three grand a trick, is in business for herself with three other women, two of them dykes, and not only does she not get bothered by the pigs but they actually set her up with some of her best clients, diplomats and foreign dignitaries and shit like that. Check it out. This woman is smart. When we talk she makes my mind do the same flip-flops my belly does when she touches me so deep. Turns out she used to be a college professor of philosophy at some fancy school back east. Says she loved teaching but that the academic bullshit she had to put up with messed with her spirit. She says it keeps everything cleaner to fuck with your body as opposed to your mind. And the money's better, too. Hell, I'd have gone to school if there were teachers like that but hey, check it out, here we are. And, girl, I am learning some things from this woman.

Besides all that, she has one whole wall of her apartment built into bookcases and they are filled, floor to ceiling, with books I haven't ever gotten my hands on. Like I said, I have died and gone to heaven. I tease her (but I'm not joking) and say that she is never gonna get rid of me till I've read every one of those books on her shelves. She kisses me so sweet I forget we're having a word kind of conversation. Then I see she's looking at me with those eyes that are more sad than sparkly, eyes that I call her "see ins" (which is what I think her initials really mean) because they see right into my heart and so far in the past and the future and right through the belly center of the present. Don't nobody else see things like C.N., which is one of the many reasons nights have turned into days into weeks and months and I am loving this woman like I actually know some things about loving in this world.

"Honey," she says. "You know that everything I have is yours. That's just how it is. You can read me, you can read my books. But I'm going to have you start over here with Sartre and some existentialists, because I have a feeling that before you get through with the Marxists you may not want to be hanging out with a bourgeois hooker and I'm not ready to let go of you yet."

I don't have a clue what she is talking about or why she thinks I could ever begin to think about leaving her. I don't know too much about Marxists or that bourgeois shit and I can't imagine what could be wrong with screwing the rich—they got the money, right? But I have learned a few ways to get that old sadness out of her eyes and so I pull her down on top of me and let the world just drift away for a little while.

we are the women

we are the horses who know no reins. no metal cuts into our cheeks. no leather pulls and jerks our heads. our direction lies within, and our bodies know the way. no sweaty straps cinch into our girths. we will bear no saddles for those who have forgotten how to ride. we run together, turn as one. strong hearts set deep in broadened chests. cresting hills, our nostrils flare to take in scent and breath. we are the women who ride the horses who know no reins. bare upon their backs we eat air with our laughter, comb our hair with the wind. our hands are free for loving. stroking warm fine necks, fingers wrapping into mane. we ride together, turn as one. bodies leaning forward, surging over hills, turning with the mere muscled press of a soft inner thigh, shifting slightly back to slow the wondrous pace. we are the women who lie down in moonlit meadows, nuzzled into sleep with dreams of thundering hooves and hearts galloping in the night, dancing circles around our bed of gathered grasses. we wake to touch in wonder the dawn-filled hoofprints embedded in the earth—protective rings around our love, left by those who know no reins.

Universal Studios

C.N. pulled into the back lot of Universal Studios and waited while a stagecoach and fifteen rangy horses passed by. A cowboy drinking a Coca-Cola and listening to a Walkman tipped his hat to her. "Can I help you find something, pretty lady?" he asked, leaning up against the side of her convertible.

"I seriously doubt you would have any clue as to what I'm looking for," she answered, putting the Trans Am in gear.

"Well, if you don't find it, you come on down to Studio 13 and I'll be waiting for you," he called out as she pulled away, driving around the horse dung.

C.N. turned down Avenue West and drove slowly through the set at Studio 9 in case Fernando was still working on his made-for-TV remake of Dickens's *Great Expectations*. The set was empty; a door banged against an old Elizabethan storefront, blown about by the Santa Ana winds. She shivered and headed over to the Costume Warehouse, parking by Jason's pink Corvette.

"C.N., darling, how are you?" A tall, slim man climbed down from a sliding ladder and dusted off his hands. "It's been forever. How are you anyway, sweetheart? What brings you to this part of town? Want to be someone else? Want to be the someone someone else desires? Talk to me, baby. You're in my house now. You can be anything you want here."

"Do I know you?" she asked, leaning her right cheek toward his kiss. "Where's Jason? I saw his car out front."

"Jason's home sleeping last night off." The man winked. "I'm his other."

"His other?" she asked.

"Yes, you know, as in 'significant other,' 'sig-o,' 'wife.' And, yes, you do know me, although not as well as I know you. Obviously. I'm James." James held out his hand, almost as if he expected her to kiss it. She briefly shook it and let go. His hand was soft and a little clammy. He continued talking. "And you, you are a living legend around here, darling. You were the star." Jason grabbed a low-neck lavender gown, edged in translucent sequins. "Here it is, darling. It's you—you are truly the star," he said, holding the gown up to her body.

"No, James. I'm the one who fucks the stars, remember," C.N. corrected him, stepping away from the gown.

"Or pretends to," James smiled, raising his eyebrow.

For years C.N. was one of the women the agents called when their leading man was leading other young men astray instead of fulfilling the duties of a handsome heterosexual hunk. She'd show up, get outfitted in new gowns, hairstyle, and identity, make a few public appearances—the new mystery woman who came out of nowhere—schedule a few photo ops for *People* magazine, reassure the studios their golden boy was a true blue woman-wanting machine. Then, after things settled down and the girls were screaming again and the actor was back on the *Cosmopolitan* most eligible bachelor lists, she'd move on to the next PR nightmare, put on a different wig and gown, drape herself on his manly arm, gaze at him with desire as the flashbulbs went off around them. Easy money, and the heterosexual façade once more patched together.

C.N. walked down the aisle, brushing past pirate costumes, ballroom gowns, corsets, slinky nightclub dresses, top hats and tails. James picked up a milkmaid's skirt, held it against his waist, gave a twirl. *"Fiddler on the Roof,"* he said. "Can you tell?" She kept walking. "C.N., darling," James whined. "Talk to me. Tell me what you need. I can make you into whoever you want to be."

C.N. stopped in front of a dressing room mirror, looking at the strange woman looking back at her: blonde—for now—good-looking, not bad for thirty-two. She stood there for a moment, wishing she could read the desire she saw in that woman's eyes, wishing that woman wasn't her. "I'm looking for something, James," C.N. said, turning to walk back to the car. "Give Jason my love."

She drove out of the studio and down Lankershim Boulevard, turning right on Barham. A few miles ahead on the left was Jimmy's studio, Stud City. She pulled into the lot, nodded at the parking attendant, and eased the Trans Am in next to Jimmy's black El Dorado. The on-camera light was on but she walked into the studio anyway, adjusting her eyes to the scene.

The lights were low. A huge hookah pipe stood in the center of the room, smoke curling up. Madras bedspreads were hung around the room. Lava lamps bubbled. On a low table next to an ashtray, a small brass dancing Ganesha figure stood, balancing on one leg, his elephant trunk covered in sequins, his four arms and wrists adorned with bracelets. The floor was covered with mostly naked bodies, groaning in a drug and sex-crazed stupor. C.N. shook her head. She knew they were supposed to sound like they were in orgy heaven, but their cries sounded like cattle mulling about, waiting for grain.

C.N. came up behind Mike, the cameraman, shooting down into the love fest, and pulled a pack of Marlboros out of his back pocket. "Hey," he whispered. "Get out of my pants, would ya, C.N."

"Hey, Mike," she said, keeping her voice low. "What's going on."

"We're just finishing up the hero comes to California scene. You know, stud comes to Hollywood, meets up with some hippie chicks, they all suck down the hookah pipe then suck down each other."

C.N. spotted Rocky, the star, sitting on a trunk over to the side, off camera. Behind him were piles of wigs, pompoms, and blue-and-white costumes. He was smoking a cigarette and holding his long, legendary penis wrapped in a steaming lavender towel. "What happened?" she asked Mike. "Somebody step on it?" He chuckled, not bothering to answer. She looked around the mass of bodies sweating and swarming on the Persian carpets, hot under the blue stage lights. "Anybody interesting?" she asked.

"Nah, not really," Mike whispered, keeping his eye on the camera view box. He panned the crowd. "Well, now that I think of it, you'd probably like the new kid, Taylor. She's too skinny for my taste, but she's got that feral, *don't fuck with me asshole* look you seem to go for." He nodded to the left. "She's down there, underneath Shawn. Skinny white girl. Long brown hair. Comes in here, doesn't talk, sits reading fucking Camus's *The Stranger* while everybody else grabs a smoke."

C.N. looked down at the girl, watched Shawn grind away on her, saw the faraway look of boredom that the camera was careful not to catch on her face. The girl's mind was clearly somewhere else. For some reason, C.N. found herself wanting to know where. The girl's slim, muscled body moved without thought under the man's weight, not even bothering to fake excitement. C.N. wondered where she went, wondered where she hid her desire, wondered if, and with whom, she let her desire be known. She thought the girl looked like she was about to pass out.

"She high?" C.N. asked Mike. Across the room she saw Jimmy reach over and turn the music up. Jefferson Airplane was singing "Go Ask Alice."

"Oh yeah," he said. "Always takes her ration of ludes and a little H before shooting."

"She with anyone?"

Mike smiled. "Down, girl," he said. "She looks like trouble, even for you. But no, I never see her with anyone. Just comes in, gets loaded, does her thing, grabs her fifty bucks, and she's outta here. I heard she's on the streets, but who knows. Nobody's seen her drive. Personally, I think she's bait."

"So what else is new." C.N. laughed. She pulled off her jacket and began unbuttoning her silk blouse. She wanted to know what that girl with no desire would feel like pressed up against her skin. She wanted to go inside her, wake her up, find where she hid her desire, flush it out. In this room of drugged and scripted sex, where no desire could possibly exist, in this girl who kept hers buried, C.N. hoped to find her own desire again. Tired of always being wanted, of so rarely really wanting, she wanted someone who did not desire her to suddenly want her. She wanted the rush of this strange girl's new desire the moment it awoke, wanted to feel that moment when she would blink, come to, slip beneath the drugs, slip beneath her mind, slip into her body's private wanting. She stepped out of her shoes, her hose, her skirt, patted Mike on the ass, and set out to find the girl.

the particulars of her emergence

she crashed through this unlocked door. bike roaring, wood splintering into my chest. frame holding. dust unsettling. quite pleased with herself, hot engines screaming. head tossed, pain throttled, glaring to be loved (they said she was too difficult). she revved her engine twice, and could have roared right on through and out my back door had she not been so very easy to love.

Let the Girl Talk

Taylor leaned back into C.N.'s arms and watched Shantelle run her tongue along the perfectly rolled joint. Diane reached over to light the thin, cream-colored reefer.

"Girl, how come you always gotta be using these straw rolling papers, anyway?" Diane asked, tucking the lighter back in her purse. "I think they taste like shit."

Shantelle took a long drag on the joint, held it for a while under a smile. She leaned her head back and struck a pose. "'Cause, girl, don't you know," she said, letting the hit out long and easy, "I just refuse to put my tongue on anything white."

Diane roared, gave her five, and reached for the joint. "Girl, you *wish* you didn't have to be putting your tongue on anything white. Don't even try and tell me those motherfuckers what come to see you aren't ninety-nine point nine percent white boys."

"Yeah, honey, ain't it the sorry truth," Shantelle said. "Of course, a girl's gotta go where the money is. And don't you know, the brothers don't need to be *paying* for this shit anyway."

The four women were gathered on C.N.'s huge round bed. Taylor felt her lover's breasts move against her back as C.N. reached over to take the joint. She wished the two of them could just be alone, but she'd learned this Sunday afternoon ritual had to play itself out. Besides, she enjoyed watching Shantelle and Diane in action. Taylor waited for C.N. to exhale and hand her the joint. Instead, she felt C.N. shift from behind her, nuzzling her ear, pulling her hair back out of her face. Taylor turned around and C.N. kissed her hard, blowing the hit deep into her lungs.

"Damn it, you two. Knock it off," Diane said. "Fucking newlyweds. Can't you see we be trying to have us a conversation here."

C.N. busted up laughing. "What's with this 'we be trying' shit, Diane? Since when did God take your sorry white ass and make you black? Why you be talking so funny lately, huh, girl?"

Taylor smiled at C.N.'s imitation of Diane's recent speech patterns. She thought C.N. sounded more like Desi Arnez doing a Rocky Balboa imitation than anything else, but what did she know. As far as she could tell, all three of the others had more ways of talking than she had even imagined possible. C.N. spoke Spanish, French, and Portuguese, and her English ran the gamut from a soft Southern drawl to a tight East Coast clip. Her accent, like her intelligence, could disappear or emerge at will, depending on her date. She mostly fucked foreign dignitaries, ambassadors, politicians, and she could play the hot and sexy Latin lover or the light-skinned, well-bred, highly educated conversationalist as she pleased, slipping the roles on and off like shoes. Usually, her dates demanded something in between—sexy without being too ethnic, just bright enough to fully appreciate the superior intelligence of the important man escorting her. Shantelle usually worked the entertainment industry and could range from slow and sultry to hot urban sophisticated chic in a snap of her fingers.

Taylor knew she was way out of her league with these women. C.N. and Shantelle both had PhDs, and Diane had just started graduate school at UCLA. Taylor had barely made it through junior high school. *Why is it all so fucking complicated?* she wondered. *Why can't people just talk like they talk?* Her heart gave a tight catch as she remembered how Jackson and Jimmy used to laugh about learning to speak "California black," and how bewildered she was when Jackson told her she didn't think, or write, the way she spoke. "I talk like I have to talk," Jackson would say. "But my thoughts are my own."

Taylor took the joint from C.N. and weighed taking another hit before passing it on. She'd lost her first hit laughing at C.N., but she didn't want to look like she was bogarting.

Shantelle reached over and took the joint from her, putting an end to her dilemma. "Hey, leave the girl alone, okay. She can talk however she damn pleases. As long as she's off the clock, that is."

Taylor wondered if Shantelle and Diane had something going on, but C.N. had told her they both were born and bred heterosexuals. Diane mostly worked the "Three C's"—cops, council members, and conventions. So far her biggest trick was with the three Japanese businessmen who'd hired her for a $7,500 all-you-can-eat package that summer—no talking, barely any fucking, they had just flown the big beautiful blond up to Pebble Beach to play golf with them for a week. Lots of photos, another grand in tips.

Now Diane blushed, a blotchy pink flush running down her cheeks and neck. "I don't know," she said. "Ever since I got back into school, I can't remember how I'm supposed to talk. Tricks are one thing, that's just a role, but this goddamn Academese just turns my stomach, makes me want to puke, makes my juices dry up just when they wanna be flowing, you know? I mean, don't all that enunciating and pontificating get on y'alls nerves?"

"Yeah, I remember that academic bullshit," Shantelle said. "Rich white boy fools babbling on and on about *problematic* this and *problematic* that, till I just wanted to grab their motherfucking throats and say, 'Hey, Jack, it ain't *problematic*. It's *fucked up*, okay. And *you're* the one fucking it up.'" She took another hit and passed the joint to Diane. "Yeah, but girl, you might as well give it up thinking you can be talking like any kind of human being if you want to get that degree."

"Yeah, I know." Diane sighed. She grabbed hold of Taylor's knee. "Hey, kid, speaking of talking, how's your new job working out? You're awful quiet for someone who gets paid to talk."

"Yeah, like anyone can say anything once you all get to going," Taylor said, wishing she'd taken that second hit. The joint was taking forever to come back her way. "Besides, I don't get paid to talk, I get paid to let the tricks talk. There's a difference." She felt C.N. smile into the back of her neck, her arms tightening around Taylor's chest. "Anyway, it's okay," she continued. "Eddie's cool, takes good care of me. The money's all right, I get whatever I want to drink, and the motherfuckers can't touch me or Eddie kicks their asses. I got no complaints."

"Hey, I'm serious," Diane said. "What do you guys talk about? I wanna know."

"Aw, man, that shit would make me crazy," Shantelle interrupted. "When it comes time to fuck, my tricks better not be trying to make me talk with them. Motherfucker opens his mouth when it's time to take care of business, he's gonna get my pantyhose stuffed in it."

Diane laughed and gave Shantelle a push. "Come on, let the girl talk."

"Hell, I don't know," said Taylor. "Mostly they just talk shit about how their old ladies don't understand them. Or their bosses. Some assholes just gotta talk about how much I look like their daughter. Once they get to going in that direction usually I gotta call Eddie. Then there's some just want to talk about their theories."

"Their theories?" C.N. asked.

"Yeah, like conspiracies. Why they don't got more money than they do. Who's really running this country. Who shot Kennedy. You know. Aliens. Economics. Shit like that." Taylor noticed Diane had let the joint go out. Damn, she thought, these girls know everything about everything except getting high.

C.N. gave her a squeeze. "Hey, baby, tell them about your literary friend."

"Well, I got this one guy, comes every day at lunchtime, stays for an hour, tips good, and all he wants to do is talk about books. It's pretty cool, really. Gives me shit, too. Books to read."

"Sounds pretty kinky to me." Shantelle laughed. "Why doesn't the motherfucker just go to the library if he wants to talk about books so bad?"

Taylor reached over and took the joint from Diane. She pulled out her roach clip and lit the joint, taking a deep hit and holding it. She felt suddenly pissed, tired. She exhaled slowly, then said, "Because everybody knows they don't let people *talk* in the motherfucking library, that's why."

Taylor felt C.N.'s body shake with laughter. Then the other two joined in, hooting, doubling over, holding their stomachs. Taylor wasn't quite sure if their joke was the same as hers. All she knew was she was gonna hold onto the joint this time and smoke the roach down to nothing all by herself until she was good and loaded and she didn't care if shit didn't make sense.

Getting Soft

Taylor woke, surprised to find C.N. curled up against her in bed, spooned into her arms, fast asleep. She felt a sharp jolt of fear. *How could I not have heard her come in?* She fought the rising panic, forcing herself to stay calm, slow her breathing. When C.N. came home after a late night of work, Taylor always heard everything—the first click of the key in the lock, the soft swing of the opening door brushing the thick pile carpeting, the rustle of her lover's coat tossed on the chair, C.N.'s sigh as she took off those too-tight six-inch heels, finally releasing tired, captive feet. Taylor would hear the tinkling of earrings and necklace, the soft velvet jewelry chest as it clicked back shut, the sound of the shower, the lathering and the rinse, the clink of the toothbrush in the glass, the silence of the floss, the soft humming as C.N. oiled her body. But tonight she'd slept through it all. *How could I not have heard her come in?* It took everything in Taylor's power to stay put, to not bolt for the door.

Around her, the bedroom was totally calm, quiet, and an almost full moon filtered softly through the skylight, casting a gentle glow. *Just chill,* Taylor told herself. *You're at C.N.'s. Everything's cool.* Taylor closed her eyes, buried her face in C.N.'s neck, and inhaled deeply, taking in the familiar scent of musk and almond soap. *She showered,* Taylor thought. *She came in, got undressed, showered and got in bed, and I didn't hear a fucking thing.* Taylor willed herself to stay still. *Damn. Maybe Trina's right,* she thought. *Maybe I am getting soft.* Taylor felt the easy yielding of the feather bed beneath her, the crisp, scented satin sheets, the warmth of C.N.'s back, pressed up against her breasts and belly. She tightened her arms around her lover's body, gently pulling her even closer. *You're really getting to me, girl,* she said silently. *Just don't fuck with me, okay? Please just don't fucking fuck with me.* Heart still racing, Taylor carefully matched her breath to C.N.'s deep, steady rhythm, and after a while she too fell back to sleep.

The next morning she woke to find C.N. up, fully dressed, standing over her with a steaming cup of espresso. Taylor looked around, confused. Sunlight streamed through the open French doors. She squinted up at C.N. *How the fuck did you get up without me hearing you?* she wondered. *Damn. This shit is not good at all.*

"Hey," she said.

"Hey, sleepyhead." C.N. smiled. "Brought you some coffee."

Taylor sat up and reached for the cup. "Thanks, baby. This smells really good."

C.N. sat down beside her on the bed and stroked Taylor's hair. "Honey, we need to talk."

Taylor felt her gut clench. *Fuck,* she thought. *Nothing good ever comes out of those words.* She searched C.N.'s face for a clue, then quickly looked away.

"Sure," she said, keeping her voice low and easy. "What's up?"

C.N. took a long drag on her cigarette and exhaled slowly. "Jackie's got a top-dollar job for me. You remember that kid she hooked me up with last month, the flaming wide receiver for the Cowboys? Well, looks like he's got himself in some tabloid trouble and needs some serious beefing up on his heterosexual credentials."

So, what's the problem? Taylor wondered. Lately, C.N. had been taking less of the traditional escort service jobs and more work providing public cover for Jackie's gay clientele, mostly movie stars and athletes. All this suited Taylor fine, because it meant that C.N. could make just as much money without having to fuck anyone. Even with all the showers and the fancy vanilla-almond soap, the smell of johns never quite washed off on the nights she had to trick.

Taylor looked up at C.N. "Yeah," she said. "I remember him." She took a sip of espresso, making sure her hands stayed steady. The coffee burned her lips and tongue, but she didn't flinch. "So, you got another date?"

"Yeah, well, it's going to be more than a date," C.N. said. "Baby, it looks like I'm going to have to go to Dallas for a while."

Taylor felt the espresso jacking up her stomach. *This isn't going to end good,* she thought. *I just fuckin' know it.* She wished she were somewhere else, anywhere, maybe catching the freight out of Santa Barbara, riding an open boxcar up the coast, or maybe just sitting down at Venice Beach, watching the waves at dusk with J. Edgar at her side. A sharp split of grief ran through her chest with the memory that J. Edgar was gone, shot dead by the pigs. She fought back the images of cops swarming the junkyard, Jimmy cuffed and bloody in the back of a squad car, Jackson boarding the Greyhound bus.

"Dallas, huh? That's cool," she said, blowing on the coffee. "If you want, I can look after your place."

C.N. looked away. "Yeah," she said. "Well, that's the problem. I'm probably not going to be able to keep the apartment, honey. They want me there for the whole season. Full throttle 'het cred.' Hot new live-in girlfriend. Serious romance. Blowing kisses from the stands. Photo ops at the clubs, bathing suit shots by the pool. Spring wedding rumors. His agent is springing for the whole nine yards." She reached over and put her hand on Taylor's leg. "The money's good, but I'm not sure I can afford to hang onto this place."

Taylor really needed to pee and felt like she was going to be sick. She wished she at least had her shirt on for this conversation, if not her boots and jeans. She needed to get air, clear her head, but she was unable to move. "So, when are you going?" she asked, trying to buy some time.

"Not for another few weeks," C.N. said. "So we've got time to figure things out. I'm going over to Jackie's this morning to meet with the agent and work out the final details, so we'll know more after that. Shantelle says you could stay with her for a while, and Eddie says she always has a room if you ever want to pick up more work."

Fuck, thought Taylor. *So everyone already knows about this except me?* She said nothing.

C.N. reached over and took a sip of Taylor's coffee. She laughed. "And, hey, Jackie says she's got a great idea. She says we should wrap you and strap you, clean you up, trim your hair, and send you out on the LPGA tour to date some of those closeted women golfers. She says those girls are already getting quite the reputation and she thinks you'd make a really cute boy date for the younger ones."

Taylor felt the room beginning to close in on her. She forced a laugh. "Yeah, right," she said. "In your fucking fantasy." She pulled back the covers and willed herself to stand. "I gotta pee."

She made her way to the bathroom, closed the door behind her, and sat down on the toilet, head in her hands. It felt good to relax, to just let go, even for a moment. She wished she never had to leave this room, never had to get up again and go back out and deal.

Taylor made herself stand back up. She slowly washed her hands, brushed her teeth, and then splashed cold water over her face. She looked around, wishing she had left some clothes in the bathroom, finding only her boxers. She knew the rest would be lying where she left them, folded on top of her bag, sitting at the foot of the bed. C.N. had cleared out a drawer and part of the closet for her, but Taylor's few belongings never had made it out of her battered old duffle bag.

She put on the boxers and walked back out into the room. C.N. came over to her, taking the girl in her arms. "Hey, baby," she said. "Listen, I'm sorry if it feels like I'm just springing this on you, but please don't worry, okay. We'll figure it out. We've got a month until I need to go, and then you can stay with Shantelle for a while and, who knows, maybe once I get settled in I can hook you up a job out there. Jackie says this guy's renegotiated Nike contract just bought him a huge new estate with an Olympic-sized pool, stables for his horses, three garages for his cars, guest quarters bigger than my apartment. You know a guy like that is going to need some help running that place." She brushed Taylor's hair back and kissed her on the neck. "What do you think, baby? Sound like something you might want?"

Something I might want, Taylor repeated to herself. *Yeah, having you leave me is just what I fuckin' want.*

"Sure, baby," Taylor said. "Sounds real good." She pulled away from C.N. and walked over to grab a shirt and pull on her Levi's.

"Okay, honey," C.N. said. "Listen, I've got to run meet Jackie. I'll only be gone a couple of hours and then we can talk more." She walked over to kiss Taylor goodbye. "Don't worry, baby," she said, stroking her cheek. "We'll figure it all out."

Taylor waited to hear the door shut and the lock click, and then lay back down on the bed, staring at the ceiling. *Something I might want,* she thought. *Something I might want. What kind of fucking joke is that?* She thought about Trina's words of warning: "Don't ever lay your burden down, girl. Trust me. It's easier that way. Once you lay it down, it just gets heavier and heavier, till one day you find it's just too damn heavy to pick back up. Better to just never set it down in the first place. Better to just keep going, one step at a time."

Taylor sighed, stood back up, and began to make the bed, fluffing up the down pillows, shaking out the comforter, smoothing down the six-hundred-thread sheets, folding them back over the blanket and tucking them tight, just how C.N. liked. *Damn, I'm gonna miss this bed,* she thought. She stripped out of her clothes and stepped into the shower, letting the hot water pound down on her body, the double massage showerheads turned on full blast. C.N.'s question continued to work at her. *What do I want?* she asked herself, feeling like the words were in some language she couldn't comprehend, or like it was a trick question on some test she'd been too loaded to study for. *I want to be back in bed and have this day start all over again. I want to be lying there holding you in my arms and your head is on my shoulder and it's a Sunday and don't neither of us have to go anywhere, and none of this is happening, or is ever gonna happen.* She let the water pound down on the back of her neck and shoulders, adjusting the temperature when the hot began to run warm, trying to catch a few extra minutes before it all ran cold. *Yeah, fool,* she laughed at herself. *You are fucking dreaming.*

Drying off, Taylor looked at the array of C.N.'s makeup, lotions, and creams sitting on the counter—night creams, face creams, exfoliants, body oils, facial cleanser, makeup remover, body-firming lotion, moisturizing pore-refining facemasks. *How does she even keep track of all this shit?* Taylor wondered. She reached for the bottle of Egyptian musk. Taking her time, she rubbed the lotion slowly into her arms, face, belly, chest, and legs, wondering if she was making a mistake carrying her lover's scent away with her.

Taylor dressed, pulled on her boots, and took one more walk through the apartment. In the kitchen, she opened the refrigerator, considered pocketing a couple of apples or maybe some cheese, but instead just shut the door, taking nothing. She turned toward the den where C.N. kept her library, but stopped, stood in the doorway, leaning back against the jam, eyes closed. She pictured the dark mahogany bookcases, always freshly dusted and oiled, lined floor to ceiling with all the incredible books she'd dared allow herself to desire. She thought about the hours she spent standing in that room, inhaling the scent of books and oiled wood, the cases taller and wider than she could stretch her arms. She thought about the nights she spent curled up reading in C.N.'s bed, waiting for her to come home, surrounded by armloads of books she'd carefully chosen from the shelves, feeling wealthy beyond imagination. *Fuck it*, she thought, turning away. *How can you carry out a whole fucking library? How would I even know which ones to steal?*

Avoiding the den, Taylor walked back into the bathroom and opened the sink cabinet where C.N. kept her stash. Crouching down, she smiled at the sight of the empty bottle of Lysol toilet bowl cleaner. Taylor knew there was easily a thousand dollars hidden inside, probably more. She remembered the time C.N. first showed it to her, grinning, saying she guaranteed no man who ever broke into her apartment was going to think of looking there. "Safer than a goddamn bank, I'll tell you that," C.N. had laughed.

Taylor shut the cabinet, grabbed her bag, and headed for the door, stopping to leave her key on the table. She wondered if she should leave a note, but what would she say? *"Have fun in Dallas. Catch you later."* Or, *"Hey, baby. I figured out what I want out of life. I want my own goddamn bed."* Or, *"I'm sorry if I'm being an asshole. You've been real good to me. I don't know what the hell I'm doing."* Or maybe just, *"I'm outta here. And don't worry, I didn't touch your fucking Lysol."*

In the end, she just left the key and walked out. As she hefted the duffle bag onto her shoulder and headed for the stairs, she thought, *Trina's full of shit. This don't weigh so much. In fact, it's light as a motherfuckin' feather.*

PART FOUR

Surfacing

birthing

who brought whom into this world? true, it's from my flesh they gather sustenance. true, it's from my hand they find their place in time. the birthing so easy it delights. souls so sweet that even as they cry and rage their bodies swell with hope and lead me to what i have not dared to ask of life. for i, too, am being born. released by babes and ancients from this middle ground to which i've clung with such tenacity. afraid to take my place within this very moment. afraid at times to even risk a breath. yet these stories take my hand as children who lead with faith and joy. i step into these vastly precise moments of mattering, where focus is fine and vision is grand. where time unclenches its whitened fist, unfolding into this soft-palmed moment where the chest expands and the earth sighs back. life inhaled deeply, mixing cellular, and exhaled as stories on a page. giving life to those who next take air. no need to spank the newborn into breath. these moments where the birthing is easy, and both writer and characters emerge.

The Shepherd and the Saint

"What the fuck do you need my name for? This has nothing to do with cops or drugs. I just got bit by a goddamn dog, okay?"

I'm pissed. My leg is killing me, I'm comin' on way too hard due to the Quaaludes I took 'cause I knew they weren't gonna give me any pain medicine at this joke of a place they call the free clinic, and now I'm getting carded. I look over at Neill. "Fuck it, let's go."

"Annie Oakley. Sir. That's her name."

Neill is the only person I know who can get away with saying the word *sir* like he means respect instead of like it's something he's trying to spit up. Which can be a useful thing around cops and I guess in certain medical situations. He knows I won't give my name to anybody in a uniform, even if it's just a sweet-faced clinic doctor, so he tells 'em what my friends have been calling me ever since I started working on the horse ranch. I've been getting a lot of shit about liking ropes and spurs and wanting something bigger and faster between my legs than what we find on the streets but that's okay. Anyway, the name Mahatma hasn't been fitting too good lately since it's getting harder and harder for me to keep on the nonviolent side of things. But right now I can't hardly walk, ride, or fight since I got my leg tore up so it's a good thing Neill is with me 'cause the clinic's the only place that will treat a minor without telling the cops and I gotta get it taken care of before I lose this job that keeps me from sleeping on the streets.

"Annie Oakley, huh?" The doctor laughs and writes something on his clipboard, which is a good sign. "I think we ought to call you Florence Nightingale. This is quite a bandage you've got here." I try and look down at my leg, but I'm not focusing too good so I close my eyes and imagine what the toilet paper wrapped up in my boss's undershirt I stole out of the laundry this morning, tied together with baling string, must look like to this guy who does this shit for a living, and then I have to smile, too.

"She got bit by a St. Bernard a couple weeks ago up at Lake Arrowhead." I listen to Neill tell the story which may be true that I made up about what happened to my leg. "She got lost and went up to the wrong cabin looking for her friends and somehow got caught in the middle when the dog tried to attack the neighbor's German Shepherd that was with her. No, she hasn't seen a doctor yet. Yeah, it's definitely infected."

Neill's voice sounds distant and hollow and I can't hardly hear the doctor, but I'm glad they're talking 'cause I don't think I can. I want to just close my eyes and sing praise for Quaaludes and self-medication 'cause now I'm feeling no pain. I think I was probably a jerk for going off on the doctor just for asking me my name but it's 'cause I felt stupid for being so fucked up the night I got bit that I don't even know what happened to my own damn leg. But pretty soon I stop even worrying about that. Fuck it. Let 'em ask the damn dog what happened.

As soon as my teeth sank in I knew something was wrong. The flesh gave way too easily, the blood tasted strange, and the cry was high and foreign. I had somehow bit into the buttery thigh

of a human instead of the thick throat of the German Shepherd
who dared approach my door with such sloppy courage, having
just come from dancing at the side of this strange girl, escorting
her out of the woods. Now I want to kill him rather than simply
teach him a lesson, so enraged I am that this young shepherd
ducked right as the human stepped amazingly left to block my
attack. But I am choking on my grief and on the blood of this
girl and know that I must tend to her now and kill or teach him
later. She enters the house and I see that she is much more than
lost and has no idea how bad she's hurt. My human is useless.
"Far out," he says, and leads her to the couch. "Here's a towel.
Want to get high?" I lap up her blood for what seems like hours
and then I see that she is about to pass out. She thinks it is from
the opium but I know her life is leaking out her leg and I must
stop that from happening. I lay my head in her lap, pressing my
shoulder up hard against the tears in her flesh that I have caused
in my outrage, plugging up the holes so that the rest of the blood
stays inside her body. She passes out and I press and grieve for
these hurt and wandering beings placed somehow in my care
without fur or faith of their own.

"Fuck, man. This dog's hurt. His whole fucking side is covered with
blood."

I don't know where I am or what the hell is going on. I know I've
been tripping and I'm definitely gonna buy up all the windowpane
Bobby has 'cause this shit is bad. I come out of this fucking awesome
trip, right, and there's this huge St. Bernard pushed up against me
with his head in my lap telling me he's sorry and talking to me like
he's God or some shit. His head is so beautiful and feels great in
my hands, the weight of it resting sweet and heavy into my sex and
belly. His breath is going all through my body and I feel like this
incredible love coming from him and think, what the fuck, maybe
he is God (who I don't believe in except that god *is* dog spelled

backward, right?) and then I laugh 'cause I know I'm still stoned and I smell the opium and see these hippie boys all around me that I don't know but they sort of look like the guys I came up here with except none of 'em are Bobby and then my hand touches something thick and sticky and I see the saint's coat is all covered in blood and I try to tell these assholes that their dog is hurt but I don't know if my words come out right so I try and stand up but I am matted into his blood and something tears through my leg and I'm gone again.

"No, man. I told you, I don't know how the fuck I got home. Maybe those guys got scared or smart or something and figured out where I lived. Maybe Bobby found me and dropped me off. Fucking punk. I just wish I could've made the buy before he freaked and split. That was good acid."

My leg hurts and I don't want to talk about it anymore, but I feel sorry for Neill because he feels like shit for passing out when the doctor dug out my wounds and besides, he definitely hangs on the sweet side of friendship with me. He's the kinda guy that can still cry after the pigs tear through a demonstration, leaving their spit and hate on our faces while our guts and blood coat the pavement, and who won't freak out when my anger comes out in screams instead of cries. You know, the kinda guy who you can just hold on to and rock with when it's all over and if you want to fuck and he can't get it up you can just say forget about your dick, man, just make love to me like a woman. And he will.

It's been ten days since that St. Bernard almost took my leg off and then apologized for it. I got back to the ranch just in time to start my five a.m. shift but I don't think the dog spit, horseshit, twelve ton of hay and fourteen-hour days did my leg much good 'cause it's all different colors now and swelled up like something the turkey vultures circle round. I can't drive for shit since just putting in the clutch makes me want to scream. So we go to the clinic and then Neill decides he wants to be some sort of fucking gentleman or something 'cause when the doctor tells me I might want to grab hold of something, Neill gives me his hand. When the guy starts digging into the wound I take it as long as I can and then leave to check out the ceiling. It's a trick I learned as a kid but I guess I forget to let go of Neill's hand when I go 'cause now I'm looking down at the scene and I see the doctor scrape more out and then Neill falls to the floor and I still got hold of his hand and my eyes are closed tight. I come back down into my body, open my eyes, look over at Neill and then the doctor who says, "I think you might have busted that poor fool's hand. I'll take care of it after I finish with you."

Snakeskin

Taylor spotted Dutch leaning up against the corral fence, a dusty boot up on the bottom rail, his Levi's slick and stiff with dirt. *The old guy don't even have an ass left on him anymore,* Taylor thought, making her way over to him. *Guess he's just wore it off riding all them horses.*

She felt good. Tired, but good. Like she might just be able to keep this new job. She came up quiet beside the barrel-chested, flat-butt old cowboy, unsure about interrupting his thoughts.

"I'm all finished stacking the hay," she finally said. "Got the grain all mixed up with the molasses like Mr. Gordon said, and the barn's swept good. Got the paddocks cleaned out and them five new stalls, too. Dumped all the shit out in that gully just like you said."

Dutch didn't even act like he heard her, just kept looking out into the corral, watching the new filly kicking up dust, acting all wild and foolish.

"Girl, can you rope?" he finally asked, spitting out a wad of chewing tobacco and turning to look at Taylor.

"No, sir. I can't," she said, struggling to meet his eye.

Lying to the boss was one thing, but this guy knew what he was doing. She had lied like a rug to the Gordons to get this job, bragging on all the experience she had working with horses, making up stories faster than the blinking young couple could ask her questions. She'd corralled every tale she'd ever read or seen on TV concerning horses into what she hoped was a credible proof of her worthiness.

"Just give me a chance," Taylor had told them. "I'll work hard. I ain't never been afraid of work. I'll take real good care of your horses and your nice place here and all. I'll do right by you, you'll see."

The Gordons had liked her, Tom Gordon especially, and hired her on the spot, room and board, fifteen dollars a week spending money. "She's got spunk, honey. Strong, too. I like this gal." His wife just nodded, not quite sure about this skinny girl with muscles like a boy and a mouth that wouldn't quit. When they told her to go on back home and get her gear, she could start right away, she excused herself, stepped outside, and returned with the small bag she had stashed out behind the rose bush in the front yard. A little stunned, Mrs. Gordon had shown Taylor to her room at the back of the house.

Now Taylor's heart sank as she felt the bowlegged old foreman sizing her up for real. She knew she couldn't hide anything from Dutch and there didn't seem any way into him, any weak spot for her to work a hustle on him either. Tom Gordon would be easy to handle. Taylor had seen a hundred guys like him before, seen how he had checked out her ass, unbuttoned her Levi work shirt with his eyes. That she could work. But Dutch was tight, self-contained, careful about what, if anything, he showed or let in. Taylor made a mental note never to play cards with this guy. *If* she could even keep her job long enough to get into a card game, that is.

She had been looking forward to shaking down the Gordons and their fancy rich friends. A little at a time, of course. But this guy was different. She saw Dutch look down at her brand-new Tony Lama boots, intentionally scuffed up to look not new, stolen from Bob's

Western Wear the day before her interview. Unable to be too picky about size, style, and color, Taylor just knew they were the most expensive ones in the store. She hoped they'd bring her luck. Two sizes too big for her, the red lizard-skin boots were stuffed with toilet paper and still pinched her toes. Taylor's feet already ached real bad and the day was only half over.

"Nice boots," Dutch said, rubbing his chin. Half his two-day stubble was coming in grey, the other half the color of sand, like the hair sneaking out from under his hat.

"Thanks," Taylor said. "My daddy got these for me. Real live snakeskin," she added.

Dutch's mouth twitched a little and he turned back out to the corral. "How you fixin' to bring that filly in if you can't rope?" he asked. "Boss wants her in by three. Shoer's comin' this afternoon." Dutch squinted over at her. "Now, is it that you can't rope very good or you can't rope at all?"

"Can't rope at all," Taylor said, knowing it wasn't worth it to even try to lie. "Never learned." She paused. "But I'll get you your horse."

"Well, Carl could rope a tick off a cow's butt at full gallop," Dutch chuckled. "But I can't say as it did him any good with that filly out there. He roped her, okay, but she caught him good with a cow kick when he leaned down to cinch up her girth. Split his cheek wide open, sent him packing with an ugly scar and a wad of severance pay."

"I ain't scared of her." Taylor worked a splinter loose from the top corral board, pissed that a damn horse might cost her this new job.

Dutch's creased face broke into a grin. "Ain't no shame in being a little bit afraid, girl. Horses are powerful creatures, worthy of a little mortal fear." He looked out at the dark bay filly, grazing a hundred yards out. At sixteen and a half hands, she was tall even for a Thoroughbred, still a little gangly but muscling up nice and long in the chest. Dutch had argued to keep her, even after she'd practically killed Carl.

"She's got spirit, boss," he'd told Tom Gordon. "Got a lotta heart and spirit. You'll need that at the track. I knew her daddy. You just can't cowboy horses like that. That's where Carl went wrong."

Dutch noticed that the filly was keeping a close eye on the two figures by the fence. Turning to Taylor, he said, "Well. You go on back to the barn now and get yourself a halter and a lead rope. Guess we better see what you can do with that wild gal out there. I'm going to go take me a siesta."

Taylor walked back to the barn, wishing she could get out of the damn cowboy boots and back into her wide-toed black street boots. "Why they gotta make these things so damn pointy?" she grumbled. "Probably so they can kick their damn stupid horses," she answered herself, grinning at her own joke. She pushed open the heavy wooden door and entered the warm, sweet, hay-smelling darkness, wishing she could just stay inside for a while and take her own siesta. That morning, when she had stacked the two new tons of alfalfa, she'd left a place in between the top bales where she could curl up and hide, or sleep, if she needed to. Taylor knew to make sure she always had a few good places to hole up.

She ducked through a side door and headed over to the row of brass-plated hooks lining the tack room wall. A bright green halter and rope hung beneath the filly's nameplate: "Fancy Dancer," out of "Shall We Dance." Mrs. Gordon had told Taylor that Shall We Dance had been a seven-time winner at Santa Anita before pulling up lame and getting turned out to stud. They had high hopes for his daughter. "Fancy Dancer, Pain in the Antser," Taylor grumbled, reaching for the halter. She tossed the lead rope over her shoulder and headed back out, stopping at the grain bin to fill her pockets with the hippie food she'd just learned rich people fed to their horses. *If I gotta be out there chasing some damn horse,* Taylor thought, *I'm damn well gonna bring me something good to eat.*

Taylor walked down the row of paddocks she had shoveled clean that morning, noticing that they all had steaming piles of fresh manure. The horses came up to the fence, curious, expectant. "What do you want from me?" Taylor growled. "Is this how it's gonna be? I feed it in one end and shovel it out the other? Three times a day. What a life." Her boss's trail horse, Rusty, the old paint gelding in the end corral, gave a soft nicker as Taylor approached. She stopped to stroke his neck and rub behind his ears, hesitating before climbing into the corral with the wild filly. "Hey, why don't you just tell your girlfriend over there to come on over," Taylor asked the gelding. He nuzzled her pockets for grain.

Taylor looked around to see if anyone was watching.

"Hey, maybe you'd let me practice this halter contraption on you a couple times before I try it on Miss Wild Thang out there." She unhooked the halter's throatlatch and slipped it up over Rusty's head, catching one of his ears, tangling up his forelock. He pushed her chest softly with his head, protesting. She pulled his ear clear, tucked the headpiece down into the bridal path, and buckled the throat strap, straightening Rusty's mane. "Damn, this thing is a lot harder to put on a real live horse head," Taylor said, stroking Rusty's neck.

The day before her interview she'd hitchhiked out to Calabasas Feed and Tack and practiced for an hour putting halters on the plastic life-sized model of Roy Rogers' horse Trigger. But Trigger stood still. Getting this halter on a moving target was a tricky operation.

Taylor practiced a few more times with Rusty till she had it pretty well figured. "Well, old guy, thanks for lending me your sweet old head. Guess I'd better go try this on your girlfriend over there."

Fancy Dancer grazed in the next pasture, keeping an eye on the girl.

"Hey, Fancy Schmancy," Taylor called out, climbing into the corral. "Let's get this over with so I can go back to bed." The filly raised her head, watching the girl approach. Taylor moved slow, humming a Rolling Stones song, swinging the halter in her left hand, holding the lead rope in her right. When she got within twenty feet of the filly, Taylor stopped, unsure. She stood facing the filly. "Please don't make this difficult," Taylor pleaded.

She held out the halter, raising it up in what she hoped was a beckoning gesture. Fancy Dancer tossed her head and bolted across the field, stopping a few hundred yards away. Taylor cursed and followed after her. Again and again the horse let Taylor get within fifteen or twenty feet of her and then took off, just out of range. Taylor limped after her, cursing.

Taylor began to sweat in the low winter sun. She wanted to cry. She wanted to shoot the damn horse or at least kick it with her stupid pointy cowboy boots. Her feet were killing her and she could barely stand up. The filly wasn't even out of breath. The girl and the young horse faced one another, about thirty feet apart, both braced, ready for the next thing. Taylor wished she had a rope, wished she knew how to cross the distance between them, wished she could somehow just fling out a circle of rope and have it land easy on the horse's neck like they did in the movies, pull her in, have something work for a change. She wished she didn't need this job so bad, wished she didn't feel it was all slipping away from her. Taylor took in a deep breath and started walking slowly toward the filly. When she got within ten feet, she stopped, and slowly raised up the halter. Fancy Dancer bolted.

"Goddamn stupid piece of shit horse," Taylor yelled, throwing the halter after her. "Goddamn worthless mule. Why you fucking with me like this?" Taylor ran after the horse, picking up the halter, waving it in the air, chasing the horse away. "Go on, run away. See if I care. Just get the fuck outta here."

Taylor ran, stumbling, crying, shaking the halter, swinging the lead rope over her head, driving the horse away. She fell to the ground, exhausted, beyond tears, wondering what would happen if she just laid there, never got up.

When Taylor finally looked up, the filly had circled back around behind her and was pacing back and forth, head low to the ground. Taylor slowly raised up to her knees, trying to keep her eyes low. Fancy Dancer raised her head, facing the girl. She flared her nostrils and snorted loudly, scaring the shit out of Taylor who had never heard such a thing. Taylor stopped, stunned, really noticing the filly for the first time. A tall, glossy bay, Fancy Dancer was almost black, her dark brown coat shiny, steaming in the cool air. Her mane and tail were jet black, as were her legs, except for a white sock on her front left fetlock. Her forehead was broad with a white lightning streak across it; her eyes, which Taylor saw clearly now, were large dark pools, filled with intelligence and spirit. "Damn," Taylor said. "Who are you, anyway? You are so fucking beautiful."

The filly widened her eyes and snorted again, sniffing for danger. Taylor reached out her hand and the horse bolted, hooves pounding, sending clods of dirt flying. This time, though, she circled tight around Taylor, keeping her inside ear up, open and flat, listening. Taylor stood still, in awe of the creature's beauty. She watched the filly's shoulder muscles lengthen, then contract with each stride. The young horse's uncut mane blew wild as she ran, her breath steaming the cool air.

"Yeah, you go on ahead and take off," Taylor told the filly. "I don't blame you. People chasing after you all the time, running you down with ropes and halters. Why the fuck should you let me catch you, anyway?" Taylor took a deep breath and let it out slowly. "It sure would be nice if you did, though. If I lose this job, I gotta go back out on the streets and there ain't nothing but trouble waiting for me there. You think you got it bad here, shit, you oughta check out the streets. Here you just gotta stand around, look pretty, get hay thrown at you, and only every once in a while have some clown with a rope come in and mess with you. Out there, *everybody* be trying to mess with you, every minute of the night and day. Mess with you in ways you didn't even think was invented yet."

Taylor looked down at the ground. The filly lowered her head, relaxing her neck. Taylor saw the movement and raised her eyes quick back to the young horse. Fancy Dancer jerked her head back up, tensing her neck, ready to run.

"I'm not gonna bother you none, girl. I already decided that. It's okay." Taylor turned her shoulder to the filly and looked back toward the house. "Coulda been a cool job, too." As the girl turned away, the horse moved in toward her a stride or two. Taylor looked back in surprise and the filly stopped, tensing. "You're kind of curious about me, aren't you, girl?" Taylor asked, her voice low, soothing. She lowered her gaze to the horse's neck and noticed Fancy Dancer relax again. "Okay, we got something going here. Maybe you're not so tough after all. Maybe you're just like me and all them other punks. Acting all tough on the outside, playing like don't nothin' matter, then movin' in to check shit out when we think no one's looking."

Taylor kept on talking, keeping her voice low and easy, watching Fancy Dancer for clues. On a hunch, Taylor turned and started slowly walking away. The filly began to follow her. Taylor turned back to face her. The young horse stopped, ready to run but not running. Taylor saw the horse's mouth relax, making small chewing movements. Its eyes were wide, ears forward, alert. Taylor turned and continued walking away, Fancy Dancer following close behind. She turned and walked in another direction and the horse kept following her.

"Damn, I was right." Taylor laughed. "I think you're just like me. I think you want some company. You just don't want somebody chasing after you, all rude and all. Hell, I don't want that either. Only difference is, you're a better runner than me. Me, I just gotta stand my ground and fight the motherfuckers." Taylor looked down, kicking a little hole in the dirt with her boot. "Dammit, see, that's why I don't want to go back out there. Somebody gonna get killed. You understand?" Fancy Dancer pawed the ground a couple of times, then took a few steps toward the girl.

Taylor's breath caught. She turned and looked up at the filly. Fancy Dancer startled, tensed up, ready to run. Taylor looked away. "You don't like me looking straight at you, do you, girl? Yeah, I can understand that. I seen people like that before. Billy, this friend's pimp I know, you just try and look at that guy any way but below his chest and that sucker'll pull a knife on you quicker than you can spit. Hates people looking in his eyes."

Taylor sighed. Out of the corner of her eye she saw the filly watching her, head low, mouth chewing, relaxed again.

"So you like it when I talk, huh, girl? Okay. I can keep talking. That's one thing I know how to do real good." Taylor talked low, keeping her eyes away from the filly. She crouched back down and tore off a small branch of chaparral, pinching off the thin needle-like leaves. "So, what you want to know, anyway? Wanna know my pitiful life story? Wanna hear how I fight the bums out behind Montgomery Wards each night for the privilege of sleeping in a cardboard box? How I raid the dumpsters for food? How every night I wake up to find some guy's dick poking round me, looking for a hole? Nah, that shit don't matter. I can take care of all that."

Taylor felt the filly move in closer.

"Okay, you probably wanna know what I *can't* handle. Besides you, that is. I'll tell you what I can't handle. I can't handle that I'm turning out just like them. I can't handle that the other night I almost killed someone. No, I can handle that. What I can't handle is that I almost liked it. I was getting ready to blow this trick in his El Dorado down on Sunset, had the clown's money and everything, hands on his pants, ready to go when the asshole starts talking about how much I look like his daughter. Now, I've heard that shit a hundred times before, but somehow this time it just works me and then the motherfucker puts his hand on my tit and starts calling me his little girl and next thing I know I got my knife up against the john's throat, screaming at him, 'If you ever touch your daughter again I'll kill you!' I watch his face get all pink and blotchy, eyes bulging out, his fear stink filling up the car, piss leaking out, staining his fancy pants, staining his fancy leather seats and I want to cut the motherfucker so bad it hurts. You understand? I *want* to do him."

Taylor snapped the branch and looked over at the filly. Fancy Dancer was about ten feet away, head down, moving closer. Taylor kept her shoulder turned from the filly, her eyes down a little. She stayed totally still, silent, and let the horse approach her. Fancy Dancer came slowly up, a step at a time, till Taylor could feel the filly's hot breath blowing on her cheek. The filly lowered her head, nuzzling into her shoulder. Taylor slowly let out her breath. She felt Fancy Dancer's lips pulling at her pocket.

"You like this hippie food, too?" Taylor asked real soft, slowly reaching for the grain. She pulled out a handful and let out a small sigh at the feel of horse lips soft against her palm. Taylor raised her other hand up and began to gently rub the filly's neck. It felt warm and solid. "Girl, this might just work," she sighed, moving her hand up, stroking the crest of Fancy Dancer's mane.

Taylor moved away a few more times, letting the horse come to her, giving her grain, stroking her head and neck. Keeping her voice low and easy, Taylor picked up the halter and began to rub it against the filly's neck, letting her smell it, nuzzle it, mouth it.

"That's it, girl. Easy now. I'm just gonna slip this on over your head. We gonna be friends. You gonna help me keep my job and I'm gonna make sure nobody else messes with you. Easy, girl." Taylor slipped the halter on Fancy Dancer, buckling it quickly under her neck, still rubbing her head, talking easy.

Taylor began walking toward the house, the young horse following close behind, nuzzling her right shoulder. When they got close to the paddock area, Taylor clipped the lead rope on, again letting Fancy Dancer smell and mouth it first. The horse stayed close, the lead rope slack. Taylor saw Dutch standing on the front porch, pointing her out to Mr. and Mrs. Gordon. She tried not to limp as she walked the last few hundred feet up to the fence.

The Gordons came up to the corral, looking in awe at their transformed horse, the filly tucking her head into Taylor's back, nuzzling her shoulder. "How did you ever do that?" Mrs. Gordon asked. "That horse has been wild since the day we got her. No one has been able to even get a halter on her. She just about killed Carl, you know."

Taylor looked down. "Aw, I don't know." She shrugged. "Just something I was born with, I guess. Yeah, I got me a pretty special way with animals. We speak the same language. Maybe it's something I picked up from my daddy. He was real good with horses, too, you know. He had him a bunch of 'em back home. Yeah, guess I just got me a natural gift."

Taylor noticed Dutch sitting on the porch rail, laughing, shaking his head, shuffling some cards, catching her eye.

# of species, class & gender

a neighbor called today. she said she'd seen tracks. she said a rancher across the valley had seen two mountain lions mating. she said she'd called in her cats, her child, her dog, and that we should do the same. i watch as her dog, a large, standard-bred poodle, dances away from her call. white, ethereal, absurd against the chaparral, he floats off into the hills. down the road mr. decker tells how a lion killed a doe right out in his apple orchard. "i didn't know a deer could scream so loud," he said, shuffling out some hay to the two spotted fawns standing wobbly legged under the trees, nibbling on fallen fruit. refusing to leave the place they last received their mother's nuzzle.

across the canyon the lioness lies down with her mate. tawny coats sprawled into the dried brown bed of grass, still hot and wet from their lovemaking. the lioness stretches and begins to lick her paws her face her belly. now, leisurely licking her sex off her lover's face, she pauses, catching strange scent. lip curled, smelling flea powder, smelling flesh, she listens as breaking twigs announce arrival. soon a floating white apparition trots stupidly into the clearing. coifed and clipped, balls cut and brains bred out, stomach filled with kibbles and bits of horsemeat, chicken, lamb. the neighbor dog blinks, and thinks about barking. in the split second between lick and leap the lioness gives thanks this day for being twice blessed.

Connections

Limekiln Creek, Big Sur: I get picked up hitchhiking by a slick silver-haired TV exec in a bronze Mercedes convertible. He pulls over, top down, flashes his perfect teeth L.A. producer smile, and asks if I need a lift. His wraparound shades prevent me from seeing his eyes, but I know who he is. Golfer, tennis tan, two kids, trophy wife, probably fucks his maid. I get in, tilt the heated leather seat back as far as it goes, and gaze up at the towering redwoods, arcing sunlit patterns against the bright August sky. I breathe deep, lungs happy to be free of L.A. smog, taking in the rich scent of warmed redwood duff and salt sea air. He doesn't bother to make conversation, but somewhere past Garrapata Beach says, "I'm stopping at the Highlands Inn. Would you like to stay with me tonight?"

I note his silk shirt, Rolex, khaki slacks, Italian loafers. He seems relatively clean and I'm pretty sure will have something worthwhile in his wallet. "Do they have a restaurant?" I ask.

Months later, turns out I'd be living with two feral dogs in a small cabin up behind the Highlands Inn, paying $35 a month rent. I get a job as a maid at the Inn, making $3.75 an hour. After watching me for a week, Pilar, the head of housekeeping, pulls me aside.

"Taylor," she says. "You are a good worker. Strong. No mess around. Soon, the boss, he will tell you he wants you to do 'something extra' sometimes for the guests. When he say that he means nasty things." Pilar makes the same disgusted tsking sound Enrique's abuelita used to make at the TV when she watched her telenovelas. "Look at me," she says, taking my face in her hands. "You are a pretty girl. A good girl. I strongly suggest you try to tell him no."

Later, vacuuming the east wing rooms, I still feel the warmth of her kind hands on my cheek and I wonder what she sees in me. *Girl. Good. Pretty.* Two weeks later, when old man Hambley comes to me, I politely decline his offer, mostly because I know I can make way more hustling on my own. Still, Pilar's words hover around, haunting me. And of course, I lose my job. But I don't mind. I tuck her words into my heart's pocket and take a job delivering newspapers out in Carmel Valley.

Perfect

It has been a perfect night out, and when she asks if I'd like to come home with her I say, "Oh yeah." We barely make it through the door before clothes start coming off. Her boots. My shirt. I fumble with her bra, pants slide down, and then there we are pressed up all hot and heavy against each other and I blessedly leave my mind behind and fully inhabit my body, breast to breast, belly to belly, my heart exploding with the relief of being called home.

Then she reaches for my ass to pull me in even closer and suddenly I feel her body stiffen, hands frozen, touching but no longer really touching me at all. I fly back into my head and think, *Oh shit! My ass. I fuckin' forgot to warn her about my ass.*

Ever since I was a toddler my butt has been deformed, mostly on the right cheek, but a little too on the left which only has a few scar lines and dimpled pockets of hardened tissue. That left cheek can sometimes pass, but the right is the game stopper, a mass of inch-deep scar tissue, hard as an old baseball, such a major lump of unyielding mass there is no way it's gonna get by as simply a nice, firm, Buns of Steel kind of ass.

No. It stops lovers in their tracks and then, more often than not, the night is shot. "What the fuck!" some say. "Honey?" others ask, trying to sound caring and not freaked out. "What happened?" The pity is always worse than the disgust, which I can handle with a laugh and a joke and then we can still get back to fucking. But pity blows the whole thing. True tenderness can sometimes work, but it will still be a long path between first discovery and down-the-road lovemaking. If we are both drunk enough, we can sometimes get by with the "Let's just pretend she didn't notice my mutant butt and I didn't notice her noticing." The worst is when she asks, "Baby, what happened?" and then I tell myself I really have to get my story down because the shame of not even knowing what happened to my own damn ass is way worse than whatever story I would or would not share.

One girlfriend who sticks around encourages me to get it checked out. "Does it hurt at all?" she asks. I like that she's not afraid to really feel around the scars. I tell her no, that it's mostly dead inside, but that lately it's started to really ache way deep down. "I wonder if it's that thing they call body memory," I suggest. "You know, trying to surface."

"Body memory," she scoffs, laughing. "It's probably fucking cancer. Honey, you should get that shit checked out."

The doctors aren't any help. "I don't know," one says, feeling around on my butt. "Could be the result of repeated blunt force trauma, but it would take months, even years to build up such deep scar tissue. My best guess is this started when you were two or three." Another thinks the scars are from repeated burns. The attending nurse says, "Doctor, do you think this could be from hot oil? There appears to be an almost splashing pattern to the scars." He prods around. "Yes, I see," he says. "But that wouldn't account for the depth of the central scar mass. See this major site? It has to be at least a solid inch deep." He takes a biopsy, suggests I get an MRI to rule out a tumor. Mostly, he just shakes his head, says, "Damn, I just don't know. I can't even imagine who or what could have done this to a child."

The MRI and biopsy reveal that there is no tumor, only the suspected deep mass of layered scar tissue. The lab technician says, "I've never seen anything like this. Do you know what caused it?" I do not. I know most of my body's scar stories, but this one has remained staunchly mute all these years. Not a word.

My memories are sketchy. I know I was hurt. I know there was terror involved. I know it was my mom. I do have fleeting images of a blood-slippery bathtub, me scrambling like a terrified animal, futile, mad with fear, but it's possible that memory comes from another time.

Once I ask my mom's old boyfriend what he knew about my butt. He remembers the scars, so I feel hopeful. "I know your mom said it happened when you were really little," he says. "I remember taking you to Dr. Rubell, and I remember your butt's been like that ever since." He pauses. "You know, I don't think we ever really knew what happened."

A year before she died, I asked my mom what she remembered about my ass.

"Was I born like that, or did something happen?" I ask.

"Oh no," she says. "No. You were born absolutely perfect. A perfect little baby."

"Well, then, what happened?" I ask, not believing I'm really going to enter this territory with her.

She looks away for a long while and then softly says, "Oh, the shame. I didn't think I would ever learn to live with the shame."

My heart stops and I think *Can this really be happening? Can we really be in a moment when truth is going to be spoken in this damn family? Is my mom really going to admit that she knows how bad she hurt me? And that she feels remorse?* My heart starts up again, excited, and I force myself to breathe. Then I see her light a cigarette and take a deep drag. She strikes a pose, cigarette in her right hand, the back of her left dramatically pressed against her brow, and I know she's flipped into some Hollywood actress and I might as well just walk away right then and there. But I don't.

She continues. "Never have I felt such shame and never will I forgive myself for what was done." I rack my brain. Who is she? Joan Crawford? Deborah Kerr? "It was that day I took you and your friend to May Company and you two just wouldn't stop acting up." She shakes her head. "You were normally such a good little girl, so happy, always smiling, never any trouble at all, but this day for some reason you just kept acting up. And so I didn't want to, but I just trotted you two out of the store, went to the car, pulled off my shoe and paddled your little fanny with the soft flat part of the slipper." She took another drag on the cigarette and looked off into the distance. "The shame," she says. "I didn't think I would ever learn to live with the shame."

This time I do walk away, angry that once more I've let myself get played for a chump. "Fanny," I mutter. "Who the fuck says shit like 'fanny' anyway?"

Gettin' Schooled

After three tiring weeks of having the small-town cops harass me and roust my van each night at three a.m. after my night shift at the Seaside Jack in the Box, I paid a local lawyer two hundred bucks to walk down the street and have a neighborly chat with the Carmel police chief. They spoke for about five minutes, gave each other a good-ol'-boy clap on the back, and told me I had a choice of county jail or community college. They knew I wasn't guilty but were trying to get me to roll on the small-town rich boy junkies who were, but that wasn't going to happen. I told them I thought you had to be eighteen to go to college and they laughed and said, "So, tell 'em you are," and then they clapped backs some more and I took their deal and walked out thinking about the only other profession I knew where you could make two hundred bucks in less than ten minutes' time.

So I went to the Monterey Peninsula Junior College, and signed up for an Abnormal Psych class taught by a wannabe charmer named Jim Lafayette who would gain world renown for killing his pretty young wife and leaving their toddler wandering alone through the Oakland airport as his coward daddy fled to France. But that was years later. For now, Dr. Lafayette was just a bright, tousled-hair young therapist who taught night classes on the side and fucked his female students whenever he could.

But I didn't know that then, and so I sat in class, totally engaged and lively minded, wondering why so many students would rather sleep than listen to this world full of incredible ideas being tossed out like candy, almost for free. Like a thief, I'd gather these bright morsels from the air and take them home like tender, stolen bones to gnaw on at my leisure. And I'd feel my mind working overtime, curious and sparkling, and wonder if maybe Jackson had been right all along when she said I was smart enough to go to college.

But I was just a chump who didn't recognize the age-old hustle in its dressed-up academic form, and so when the teacher handed me back my first paper, told me how impressed he was with my brilliant analysis and how he wanted to hear more about my unique perspective and innovative theorizing, I actually thought he meant it. And I felt so special when he invited me over to his apartment for a study session with other "bright-minded students" to talk more about these concepts. *Yeah*, I thought, feeling shy and a little smug. *Maybe Jackson and C.N were right after all. Maybe I am kinda smart.*

And so I went to his apartment that night feeling all giddy and nervous and excited and I didn't even catch on when I walked in and saw that there were no other "bright-minded students" there, just low lights and easy jazz playing soft in the background. And then he offered me a glass of wine and told me how he loved my long hair and it all became suddenly, sickeningly clear. And then, when he showed me his gun, lovingly stroking it and setting it down on the credenza for show, I almost laughed out loud. *Ha! You motherfucker!* I thought. *You goddamn motherfucking rapist trickster son of a bitch. You really had me going there. And I thought you were a person! Ha! You ain't nothin' but a motherfucking trick without a car.*

I looked at him standing there in his tan corduroy trousers and beige velour shirt, open at the neck, and saw how weak he was, how easy he'd be to take out. I saw the soft belly, how easy it would be to bring him down with a quick knee to the groin, how fast his own knee would give way with a simple cow kick from the side, how his nose would gush blood just like any other asshole's with a good palm crush, not even a fist. And then, when I saw how easy the fool let me get between him and his gun, I did laugh out loud. *You're on my turf now, motherfucker,* I thought, feeling suddenly calm, happy and home. *There's no way in hell this night is going down like you think it is.*

I don't remember what I actually said that night, but I do remember that no physical violence was necessary, that my scorn and derision were palpable enough to leave him cowering against the wall as I walked past him and out the door. Still, it would be years before I set foot in a college classroom again, and when I read decades later about the young woman's murder and the toddler left wandering the airport terminals, I questioned my decision to walk away that night, and thought about how easy it would have been to just pick up the gun and do the world a favor.

PART FIVE

Secondary Drowning

Secondary Drowning

I

Every night the dreams come. The drowning dreams. The getting shot dreams. I feel like I am dying. The physical world taunts me. My weakness catches in my heart. I don't know who I am anymore, I tell anyone who will listen. But no one can. Stories crawl out from underneath one another, push apart sentences, balloon out of air, floating. But these are the stories they do not want to hear. Tell us how you met, they say. First date. Second date. Third date. Linear. Contained. Tell us about the ocean. Tell me again how you pulled Luna from the sea. I cannot breathe. I'm turning underwater. Where is the light? The bullet rips through my shoulder and I crash to the ground.

II

"Let's go camping," Leah says. "I want to be outside. I want to move my body. I want an adventure." In two weeks she will return to graduate school. My boss has given me a few days off, so we load up my truck with sleeping bags, a tent and camp stove, firewood and groceries, leaving a spot for Leah's dog Luna to curl up in the back. Shen, my white-faced Golden Retriever, will stay behind, too old for an adventure. She lies down by the barn, indignant but resigned, her head resting on crossed paws, waiting for the truck to pull away without her. My cat sits on the fence post, cleaning herself, waiting for the mourning doves that come each day to steal the horses' grain. The sun warms the horses' backs as they finish their morning hay. Their breath, like the sun, warms the cool winter air.

Driving down the Big Sur coast, I watch carefully for animals darting across the road, deer, cottontails, skunks, quail, possum, red squirrels, looking for food, looking for water. After two dates in the city, I'm happy to show off the ranch, the coast, this part of Northern California land I now call home. I point out a red-tailed hawk circling the hillside to our left, the Odello artichoke fields on the right, Cooper's old barn. But Leah's not even looking out the window. She's reading out loud from a book she says is haunting her so bad she can't put it down.

"Listen to this," she says, all excited. "They had a secret code word for their mother's madness just like we did as kids. They called it the 'Topaz Bird.' This book is so beautiful. I've never read anything that catches the love and the loss so perfectly." She reads another passage from *Ghost Dance,* the language indeed lovely, haunting, lyrical.

Pulled into the story, compelled, I also find it irritating as hell. I wonder who this person is beside me. A mutual friend set us up, but I wonder if I have what it takes to "date." I wonder why I'm even going out with someone who pays her analyst more each year than many families live on. Still, here we are. Ahead, a young cottontail darts across the road, ducking into the chaparral. The hawk circles back out of sight.

"My mom was a writer," Leah says, finally looking out the window. "So brilliant and so beautiful. She was always very sick. I remember her in such torment, the tragic one of our family, her pain leaking out in exquisite poems, us kids always trying to keep quiet, to make it okay. She killed herself seven years ago, a year after I moved out to California."

I pull the truck off the road, shut off the engine, move my arm up to the back of her seat, lightly touching her shoulder. She answers my eyes.

"Drowned herself in the St. Charles. Left us all our own individual notes. Took a cab to the riverbank, hung her clothes neatly on a tree, parked her wheelchair, and crawled into the river. My father quietly followed the clues, gathered up her clothes, left her wheelchair, rode the patrol boat downriver, carried her body back for burial. The note she left me read, 'I have always loved you, darling. Please forgive me.'" Leah begins to cry. "I loved her so much. I could forgive her anything but that. Why did she have to ask me for the one thing I cannot give her?"

I'm not sure what to say. I can see this is a story she has told many times. We sit for a while, quiet, watching the surf far below silently pound upon the shore.

"Come on," she finally says. "Let's go check out this beach. I want to be outside." Leah jumps out of the truck, stretches out her arms, arches her back and takes a deep breath of ocean air. "It's beautiful here," she says.

"This is Garrapata Beach," I tell her. "My old stomping grounds. I used to hitchhike up here when I was a kid." Luna, a brown-black Labrador mutt with a kind and mischievous face, barks from the back of the truck, whining with relief and excitement as I open the tailgate for her. I smile in recognition, letting her off the leash. Hiking down the cliff to the beach below, I'm happy to see Leah has left *Ghost Dance* behind in the cab of the truck.

It is our third date. Leah tells me she can never get really "serious" about me because I'm not Jewish. Still, here we are. Hearts intrigued, bellies full of bagels, we walk along the white sand beach, stunned and excited as twenty-foot waves crash down upon one another two hundred yards out to sea, sending in frothy surges to beat upon the rocks, wrestle with the undertow, eventually lapping innocently up onto shore. Luna picks up a giant piece of kelp and dances it down the beach, galloping, tripping, ferociously shaking the seaweed, sending sprays of sand and water off in glistening arcs.

Leah asks me about my mother. "She was a union organizer," I say. "Great liberator of the working masses. Worked for the farm workers in the fifties before it was cool. Hung out with Cesar Chavez, Dolores Huerta. Excellent politics on the outside. Very fucked up on the inside. She almost killed us both a hundred times. As far back as I can remember. Drinking. Rage. Grief. I gave up my body to keep her alive, to keep us alive. What else can a child do?" Leah seems stunned. Not knowing how to read her look, I quickly cover my tracks. "Don't worry," I laugh. "I got outta there young, before anyone got hurt too bad."

I pick up a piece of mossy driftwood and throw it into the shallow surf. Luna bounds after it, trotting proudly with the stick in her mouth.

Waves crest a translucent silver green, then thunder down in a deafening roar. "Boy, the ocean sure is rowdy today," I say, and we burst out laughing at the utter inadequacy of the word "rowdy" to describe the magnificent sea before us. I feel young-girl shy and courageous as I reach for the hand of this curious one by my side, wondering just who she is and exactly how she came to be walking beside me this day. The sun is warm and it feels good to laugh, even at myself.

Leah speaks of the power, sensuality, and erotic intensity of the sea and I smile. Unwilling now to talk in words, I let the animal part of me growl in response, a soft, low, throaty call with lots of r's and no real g's at all. I watch the sun rest on her hair as she watches it dance on the water and I wonder what it would be like to make love with her. Ocean-charged air surrounds us. The sun is warm on my back, the whole front of my body aches to hold her close against me and I am extraordinarily happy to be in this very moment of time and place.

I am on the shore and she is with me.

We come to a rock jutting out from the bluff and debate about going on around it. There is a good chance our feet will get wet if we race the waves to the other side, and neither one of us seems too inclined to move very fast. I climb up on the rock to see what's beyond and to determine if it's worth the energy to scramble around or over.

I look down from my perch, grinning like a cougar at the ease with which I leapt up onto the rock, happy that two and a half years of college haven't completely taken all of my body strength and knowing away. The cliff feels warm, rough against my shoulder; the rock strong, solid beneath my feet. I think about taking off my old Nikes so my toes can grip rock, touch sand. I smile down at Luna and Leah. The joy I feel at the sight of this lovely, silky girl and her silky dog standing on the beach below is so palpable, as rich and dense as island air, that I find myself trying to inhale it, to take it deep inside my chest and let it just hang out with my heart for a while.

I am on the shore and she is with me.

A wave comes up a little farther than the rest and I see her laugh up at me as her purple hi-top sneakers get wet after all. The sun is warm, her feet are wet, my eyes are locked in delight with hers and I am laughing too.

Then I am completely under water.

I think, *I can't be underwater, I'm fifteen feet in the air, the sun is warm, the sand is dry…*but I'm moving up against the cliff in slow motion, half crawling, half swimming, my hands grabbing onto rocks. Salt pushes its way into my eyes and nostrils. I feel my glasses slide off my face. Someone is untying my Levi jacket from around my waist and I wonder who and why. I think of Leah and Luna on the beach below and my scream comes out a gurgling echo, stifled by the roar around me and the water snaking down my throat.

I am drenched against the cliff, clinging. The water has receded, my glasses are caught between the rocks and the V of my shirt collar. I slowly make my way back down to the rock, scared to let go of the cliff. I know better but I look down anyway at the place where Leah and Luna had just stood and I am stunned by their absence. Everything looks just the same except that they are gone, I can no longer feel the sun, and the sand is spitting bubbles. I spin around to the ocean and see two small dark dots flying out to sea. My mind screams "No!" and I hear Leah scream back, "Tay-lor, help me!"

I am on the shore and she is gone.

She is easily a hundred yards out to sea. The waves crashing behind her are making three-foot-high swells of turbulent froth, coming in from four different directions, churning against the force of the riptides pulling her back, pulling her under. The two dark dots are getting thrown around, tossed like twigs. She calls out again: "Tay-lor."

I am on the shore and she is in the sea.

She is calling me and my heart is breaking and I pray for the strength to not go in. For it is an impossible sea. I can immediately tell there is no such thing as "rescue." It is not that I am afraid of dying, just that there is no way I could possibly even get to her, much less be able to do anything if I did. She is a much stronger swimmer than I am and I can see that there is no swimming going on out there. Panicked, I look toward the road—a fifteen-minute hike and then what? Maybe a flagged-down motorist, maybe a cell phone, probably no signal anyway. It is useless. There is no help. The beach is empty. I think, *This is how people die.* I think, *She is probably going to die. And I don't even know her father.*

I see the picture she showed me this morning—her father, East Coast intellectual, tall, lanky, his dark, thick hair unruly, glasses sliding down his nose, standing in front of a well-kept brownstone, looking awkward, shy, leaning slightly away from the pale, curly headed girl holding tightly on to his L.L. Bean corduroy trousers.

I think about Leah's dear friend Susan who introduced us and then stood smugly back to watch what happened. How can I tell Susan? I think about the silence of rescue squads coming too late. I think about bodies washed up on shore. Time expands and in my mind's eye I watch dry, fully clothed firemen zip Leah's pale, limp body up into a shiny black bag and carry her up the cliff. I think about funerals, hillside burials. I see her father, stooped with grief, unable to bear this loss as his favorite daughter follows her mother into the ground seven long years later, the two great loves of his life stolen by water, drowned, this bright, lovely one leaving no tormenting notes of explanation behind.

I am on the shore and she is in the sea and there is no help.

And she is calling for me. "Taylor! Help me." Her cries tear through my body. I can't tell if she is calling my heart back into or out of my body, but I feel it breaking and I know I must respond yet I know I cannot go in or we both will die. I hear echoes of other voices that have called to me. I hear the faint childhood cries of David, the crippled neighbor boy I saved time and time again from crazed beatings until once, three a.m. on a hot L.A. night, Santa Ana winds blowing, I heard the familiar metallic sound of his head hitting the back of the wheelchair, tried frantically to think of something I could innocently go next door to borrow—sugar, cigarettes, whiskey, anything—but when I tried to get up, my skinny, ten-year-old legs went numb, dead, glued to the bed, useless as David's, and I lay there till the metal sounds stopped and then I lay there till the dawn sky broke and I heard the ambulance rush up and then drive slowly off, carrying his body away.

I am on the shore and there is no help.

She screams out, "Taylor! Help!" I think, *She is going to have to save her own life,* and then I am flooded with the understanding of how incredibly strong she is. I think, *No one else would even be alive right now and she is still hollering for me.* And in those cries for help that had moments ago tormented my very soul, I now hear the incredible breath and power they contain and I am deeply moved by her courage and will to survive. I think, *As long as she can call so strong, she is okay, she is getting air and she is fighting.* Now her cries make me happy. I feel love fill my chest, feel strangely proud of her. Hope surges through me oblivious to reason and odds and I call back to her, "Leah! I hear you. Leah, come here!" I know it is a ludicrous thing to say and that she can't hear me anyway, much less "come here," but somehow the calling back to her forms this cord of energy that I can almost see as vibrant gold-white strands of light and heat. I feel her strength and courage surge through the cord and I send back love, faith, dark earthy hope.

I am on the shore and she is in the sea

and I am calling back to her, sending her strength, pouring love and admiration down through the gold shimmering cords, telling her that I know she knows she must first save her own life and that I am making myself strong and grounded for her, that I am preparing to be as courageous as she and I will do whatever I can when it is my time. I feel the cord as a lifeline to her, yet through it I am gaining courage from her strength. The energy is awesome and I am feeling increasingly grounded, rooted and hopeful, amazed at the connection, the lack of fear. The gold-white cord is as clear to me as the blue sky, the black rocks, the white foam, the two dark dots. It pulses with the exchange of vibrant love, courage, life. I think, *How strange, in the midst of this terror such a sweet miracle can occupy the same precise moment of time.*

Then in horror I watch as the two dark dots are picked up by a huge white wave and hurtled toward a craggy, glistening rock fifty yards out to sea. She screams and I am again helpless and

she is in the sea

and I can't find either of the two dark dots and I am scouring the area around the rock, searching for sight of her. To the left I see something with dark hair floating underwater about twenty yards offshore and I dive in, swimming impossibly toward her body. Gasping air I go under to grab hold of her and then my hands clasp down and I am holding onto Luna. I open my eyes underwater and stare at the limp silky dog that looks like a furry seal. I am happy to be holding something but shocked that it is not Leah. Then I think, *Well, if she lives, she will be really happy that I saved her dog,* and I start back for shore, arm tucked under Luna's chest, swimming effortlessly with a wave which carries us both in. The dog is fine, standing on her own, sucking air, puking salty froth, shaking sprays of water and sand and

I am on the shore and she is in the sea

and I can't find her. I remind myself to breathe now that I can. I try to calm down, will myself to be able to see her. Finally I spot her far to the right of the rock. Somehow I know that she is still alive but she is not calling to me anymore and now I curse the lack of cries for I know this means she is weakening. She is closer in, but still way too far out for me to get to her. My eyes fix on her body, straining to re-establish the shimmering cord, searching for her breath. I think, *Can I really just stand here and watch someone die?*

and I cannot. I can't just stand there and watch as she dies. And I do not want to die. I do not want to fucking die. I think of all the large and small survivals, the beatings, the rapes, the johns, the pimps, the cops, the car crashes, the gay bashes, the falls, the fights, the flights, the fear. And the funny thing is, before I didn't care but now I do and I do not want to die. I do not want to fucking die. I rage and my throat fills with grief but I am at peace with my answer. I tell myself that soon it will be time and I will go in.

I am feeling utterly calm. I take off my soggy tennis shoes and socks, lay them carefully on the rock, fold and gently place my glasses on top. I think of those who will find our bodies, trying to make sense of the situation, friends coming back to the beach to search for clues. Looking at my little pile, I think, *Perhaps this will tell them of my intentionality. Maybe that will help.* My toes curl into the sand, gripping a small, gritty rock. I feel my throat constrict and swallow. Soft wind touches my cheek. I start to take off my heavy jeans so I can move less encumbered in the sea, but when I look up to check on Leah, I see that she is suddenly floating face down in the water and I run into the surf, screaming, "Leah, no!" At the same time I am sending silent apologies to those whose love has kept me so far in this world. And I am leaping, tripping, diving into this white frothy hell.

A wave slams me down and I see my mom running crookedly onto the Santa Monica Freeway. My mom's boyfriend stands stupid under the streetlights, holding her car keys, confused, thinking he had finally won a battle. I dutifully race up the onramp, tackling my mom before she makes it into oncoming traffic, grieving the asphalt I know is tearing into her face and I guess my arms. I roll us over and over until we are off the shoulder and into the dirt, rolling until the cyclone fence pushes into my back. My arms clench around her chest, pinning hers, refusing to release. I wait for the boyfriend or the sirens, whichever comes first. I don't really care. Sobs rack my mother's body, pushing into my chest. "Just let me die. Please, God, just let me die," she cries over and over, though she makes no effort to break free.

The wave pulls me under and I fight my way back up, gasping for air, searching for Leah, cursing this ocean, swimming impossibly toward the dark, bobbing head. Somehow I reach her and grab the back of her hair and yank her head out of the water, screaming for her to breathe. Her hair is like seaweed. She is blue cold like stone with popping veins etched across her brow. For a moment I see David's pale face in the open casket, dead, waxy as if someone painted it with crayons, and then I am yelling, "Leah, I've got you. I've got you now. I'm not gonna let you go!" and I am swimming with more than all my strength toward shore, fighting to keep her head above water, feeling her limp legs bump, bump into my violent kicking ones just like David's used to do at the city pool. But we are both going backward, pulled further out to sea.

I am in the sea

and cursing the ocean and screaming and swallowing water, somehow imagining I can ride my fury back to shore and save us both but instead I am thrown backward, helpless as a twig and I'm worried that Leah can't breathe and I'm not sure which way is up but I know I'm not gonna let her go and I am so angry at this ocean for making me feel my weakness. My mind makes one last grab for the rational. *We're caught in a riptide*, I think. *"When caught in a riptide,"* I hear a robotic voice say, sounding like an airline stewardess giving oxygen mask instructions, *"do not fight the current. Simply swim parallel to the shore until you are out of the riptide and then swim safely in."*

"Fuck you," I scream as we get dragged under again, spinning around, somersaulting backward desperately up for air. "There is no fucking parallel out here!" I feel my right shoulder tear as we get twisted around and I struggle to hold on to Leah, wondering if I could shift her body over to my stronger left side. But I need that side to swim and I don't dare risk such a maneuver. Mentally I make sutures in every tear the ocean rips through my muscles. At first they are stitched in golden pink filament, then twine, then rope, duct tape, baling wire, anything I can find as I feel my body break apart. I see Jo-Jo and her pink little nursing kit and whiskey, sewing us all back together. I see Mike standing under the tree in North Hollywood Park, ready to break my fall as I plummet from the sky, hollering at me to grab on to that last goddamn branch. Soon my thoughts reduce to: Hold on. Air. Up. Breathe. Shore. God?

And I am in the sea and there is no help.

The numb grip on my mind breaks and I am again fighting with everything I have. I am not calm. I am pissed off. Once a wave brings us close enough in that I can touch bottom I dig desperately in with my toes only to get swept back out again and again and I'm spitting and cursing and telling Leah that I'm not gonna let her go, I'm not gonna let the ocean take her away from me and then we get washed up far enough that I can stand and she is kneeling and I feel her gripping my arm and so I know she is still alive and I try to pick her up like they do on Baywatch and trot pectorally up to shore so we are finally safe but I can't even budge her. I use all my arm and back strength and then try to lift with my legs but my body is too weak and she is not even moving and I wonder if maybe she thinks she is finally safe because she feels sand and my arm but she is not safe so I scream at her to help me. "We have to get out of here," I yell. "You've got to help me. We're not safe yet and I can't carry you. Please, anything, just try to crawl."

My grandmother has fallen in the hall. I know what I have to do. I've done it before. Put two of the tiny white nitroglycerin pills gently under her tongue, careful so she doesn't choke. Get her to her bed. Careful. Carry, drag her if she can't help. Take her dress off, careful so it doesn't rip. Unsnap each one of the thirty clasps on her corset, releasing her chest, letting her breathe. Call the doctor. Call my mother. Call the ambulance if it's bad. I spill the bottle, tiny pills scattering. Shit. I pick up two from the orange shag carpet. "Grandma, can you hear me?" I ask, turning her head, prying open her mouth, closing it gently over the two white pills. "I'm gonna get you to bed, okay?" She doesn't move. I try and lift her. She is five foot ten, not fat but big boned, a "woman of substance." "Thick with grief," says my mom. I am eleven. "Grandma, can you help me get you up?"

I know what to do. I've done it before. Why can't I lift her now? She is so heavy. I pull her partway up the wall, then slide down after her into a heap. I want to cry. Why am I so weak? "Grandma, can you help me? I need to get you to bed." I'll have to drag her.

Slowly we make it down the hall, my grandmother waking up enough to help push with her feet. "The bicycle?" she whispers. "Do the bicycle?"

"That's right, Grandma. Just like you're riding a bicycle, only backward. Just keep peddling. I got you, Grandma."

We make it to her bedroom, but when I pull her top half up against the bed, her butt still on the floor, I feel her dress give way. Panicked, I want to run when I see the long tear under her armpit. But I make myself stay, get her into bed, pull off her dress, undo the corset, wipe her brow with a clean damp cloth first, check her breathing, then call the doctor, then call my mother, then wet the cloth again, then wipe up where she's messed herself. She breathes more easy, then starts to cry.

"Oh, child, just look at me!" she says as I tuck the sheets soft around her chin. "I came here to take care of you kids. I'm supposed to be taking care of you. Oh, just look at me."

"Shhh, Grandma. It's okay. You take real good care of me, Grandma. I love you so much. Just rest now. Dr. Mandle will be here pretty quick. Mom's comin' too," I add.

She puts her hand real gentle against my cheek, rubbing my chin with her big thumb the way she knows I like, the way that makes me feel like a cat, the way that makes me feel so good I forget to hide her dress. Then when my mom and Dr. Mandle get there of course my mom spots it right away, glaring at the tear, shaking the dress, giving me one of her *you'd better be gone* looks, but Dr. Mandle is there so all she says is, "And what happened here, young lady? I swear you cannot be trusted with anything. I don't know what I'm going to do with you. So damn careless. Always breaking things, tearing them up. I don't know what I did to deserve a child like you."

She leaves the room and Dr. Mandle looks up and says, "Don't worry. She's just upset, that's all. You did a real good job here. Your grandma's just fine." But he gets to go home and I know my mistake was settling all in to my grandma's thumb stroking my chin, making like I was a cat what could purr instead of a girl that needed to be sewing up her grandma's dress like I knew I should.

The next wave knocks me over, but I hold onto Leah, dig my feet into the sand, refuse to let it drag her back out to sea. I grab hold of the back loop of her jeans with my right hand, put my left hand under her shoulder and pull but there is no movement and now I understand the meaning of "dead weight" but she's not dead and I can't go back into that sea again and I yell to her, almost sobbing

I am so weak, "Crawl! Goddammit. Please crawl." Amazingly, she raises her head and says in this calm, soft voice, "I think it might be better if I walked." I want to laugh out loud in relief and disbelief at her actually uttering words much less suggesting walking—"Fuck, yes, please, let's walk. Hell, let's two-step"—but we are not safe yet and the ocean is still trying to steal her back. She raises up a little and I put her left arm around my neck and lift, hoisting her up on my right hip. I cannot feel my right side, but I look over and see my right hand snaked around her on its own, tightly gripping her waistband. Knowing if I fall now I won't have the strength to stand again, I carefully wobble us up onto shore, toes gripping into sand, relaxing, inching forward, gripping again.

Thirty feet from the surf, still we are not safe, pinned between sea and cliff. I close my eyes and begin a slow shuffle up the beach, cursing the thunderous crashing of waves, the roar that shakes the ground we walk on, threatening my tenuous balance. Finally we reach the place where the river cuts through the cliff and we limp as far as possible up the creek bed, away from the sea. When we are finally safe I take off all our clothes, even though Leah is wanting only to curl up and be still and is irritated as a cranky child at my messing with her stuff. Finally she is naked and I hold her up against the remaining warmth of my body, her back against my chest and belly, my arms wrapped around her, facing her toward the sun. Burgundy scrapes lace across her cool, white skin, telling stories of frantic legs, forearms braced against oncoming rocks, protecting her precious, unmarked skull. I watch the purple and gray gathering of bruises as her body warms and the blood begins to flow. Soon she will spit sand, grumble at Luna, hold her exploding snow cone frozen head, double over with cramps, and finally hobble her way behind me toward the truck, holding my trembling hand and wincing over a stickery path. But for now, she is safe and all I really know and care about is the fact that

I am on the shore and she is with me
and the sun is almost warm.

III

We spend the next three days huddled in a Big Sur hotel room,
clinging to each other, eating hot soup and crackers. Leah doesn't
want to go to the hospital; she just wants to get warm and dry. I
can tend to her cuts. Her bruises will be bruises. Amazingly, she has
taken in almost no water. Luna and I are both still spitting up the
sea. She barks each time I cough, wags her tail fiercely, leads me to
the corner of the bathroom floor where she has made her own little
frothy pools of yellow ocean. I clean up after her, then throw up
in the sink. The sign on the front door says NO DOGS ALLOWED IN
ROOM, but there is no way I am about to be separated from either of
these two creatures I've just pulled from the sea.

Leah and I begin to tell the story to one another. "It was
incredible," she says. "I could see you so clearly on shore. At one
point I saw this amazing tunnel of light coming from you, filled
with little strands of gold and silver light. I felt like you were sending
me breath, sending me a lifeline. You made me feel so strong, like I
could maybe save my own life. Before that I knew I was going to die.
I thought, 'How strange. So this is how people die.' I thought, 'I'm
probably going to die.' Funny what a drowning mind can invent,"
she says, looking away.

"I saw the cord, too," I tell her. "And it gave me hope. Before
that, I was so scared. I didn't know what to do. I started to run down
the beach for help…"

"Oh God!" She interrupts me. "I *saw* you do that. I saw that very
moment of panic. I saw you look down the beach and I just knew
if you ran I would die. That was the only time I was really scared.
That, and then the rock." She starts to tremble. "What happened?
Did I hit that rock?"

"I don't think so," I say. "At least not full on. I think maybe it parted the wave carrying you and Luna because I found her way on the other side from where you were." I tell her for the tenth time how I rescued Luna. I tell her the story of David. I tell her about how her cries called my heart back into my body.

"I almost couldn't cry out," she tells me. "It was like I didn't think I deserved that much attention. Like I didn't want to be a problem. I wasn't supposed to make noise." She pauses. "Guess I changed that script, didn't I?" she says, smiling. "It felt so incredible once I started hollering. I really got into it. It made me feel so powerful, even though I was crying for help. It was like I knew I had to save my own life. Like I really felt my life was worth saving."

"You did save your own life," I remind her. This is an argument we will have many times.

"*You* saved my life," she says, snuggling in closer to me. "You pulled me from the sea."

"A wave took you out and a wave brought us back in. And in between we got seriously fucked with." I start coughing again, feeling like I'm going to be sick. Luna jumps on the bed and begins to bark. Leah grabs her around the neck and pulls her down, quieting her.

"Well, you still saved my life," she says, ruffling Luna's fur. "I would be dead if you hadn't come in. I don't know what else you can call that besides saving my life."

"That's true, it's just not the only truth," I tell her. I make myself sound calm but really I want to throw chairs out the window, smash lamps, run my fist through the sheetrock walls. "You were out there ninety percent of the time by yourself before I could even get to you. You did everything right. You relaxed, didn't fight the current, swam only enough to come up for air, stayed calm. You called for help. You made the decision to live."

"I know," she says. "It was so incredible. I kept thinking about my mom. Ever since she killed herself, I've wondered if I was suicidal. Like way deep inside me. What I realized out there was that I really did want to live. It was so empowering. I feel like I really have a life now, like I really *own* my own life. I feel so strong." She looks down at her scraped and bruised arm and laughs. "Yeah. Kind of sore and beat up, but still really strong."

I feel weak. I feel sick with my weakness. Every night I drown again and again in my dreams, going under, losing my grip on Leah, letting go, losing sight of the light which means up, which means air. I scream in my sleep. "I'm not gonna let you go," I cry, grabbing hold of her body next to me, jerking her awake.

"I'm right here, sweetie," she says, all sleepy voiced. "I'm not going anywhere. We're safe. We're not in the ocean anymore. It's okay. Let's try and get some sleep."

Back home it gets worse. Everybody wants to hear the story. The Great Dyke Ocean Rescue Story. Some people cry. Some clap me on the shoulder. Shake my hand. Some dissolve into their own stories of loss, of near drowning. A friend of mine who knows the story of David says, "Oh, Taylor. This is so wonderful. You've broken through the old pattern of not being able to save David. This time you did it! It all worked. Here you both are! I'm so happy for you."

A friend of Leah's says, "Hey, I heard that near-death experiences make for really hot sex." She winks. "How 'bout it? Is that true?"

Another friend says, "Did you guys report this? Somebody should know about this. It's just not safe out there. I can't believe you didn't go to the hospital. You need to tell somebody. Call the police. Something."

"What are the police gonna do?" I ask, laughing for the first time in weeks. "Arrest the fucking ocean? That wave's outta here. Probably in the Bahamas by now. Besides, you know I don't talk to cops."

I lose my construction job. The sound of power tools frightens me. My hand flies back at the icy touch of steel. I drop my skill saw off a roof when it begins to whine and vibrate before I've even plugged it in. No one gets hurt. But still. I try and pick up some landscaping work. The other gardeners laugh past me and my broom, my hand clippers, my old buck saw, their chain saws, electric trimmers, power blowers ripping through the air as I crouch to slowly pat down a little patch of soil.

Two weeks later my friend gives me a number to call. She's tracked down a park ranger named Eric who is the lifeguard for the Big Sur area. Says he keeps records of drownings. Says it would be really good if I could call and give him the details. I call and agree to meet Eric down at the Point Lobos State Park. He listens carefully to the story, takes notes, frowns.

"I know that beach well," he says. "It's really dangerous. I wouldn't have gone in. You guys are really lucky. There's no way you should have survived." I look at his smooth, tanned chest, his oily, well-defined muscles, his wetsuit, fins, surfboard, orange floaty devices. He is the only lifeguard on duty from Moro Bay down near San Luis Obispo all the way up to Sunset Beach south of Santa Cruz. A hundred and eighty miles of coast. "Mostly I just bring bodies in," he admits. "I don't hardly ever get to really rescue anyone." He points out to the rough waters off Whaler's Cove. "But I practice every day out there," he says. "I swim two miles, paddle two more. I'm always ready. I just can't always get there in time."

I ask him what the hell it was that hit us, what made it go from dry sand to fifteen solid feet of water. "They call them rogue waves," he says. "Sneaker waves. They start hundreds of miles offshore. Come in like a swell sometimes, not like a cresting wave. That's what yours was. A swell that just kept coming. There's no way you could have seen it coming, nothing you could have done. You guys are really lucky."

I ask him why it was that Leah could have been floating face down and not taken water into her lungs like me and Luna. "The body is an amazing thing," he says. "It just starts shutting down. After she hit that rock she probably started to lose consciousness. She would have stopped breathing by the time you saw her floating. So she wouldn't have been taking in air or water."

Eric looks down at the breakers below.

"At that point," he continues, "you just got three or four minutes to get to the person before there's irreparable brain damage due to lack of oxygen. Obviously you got to her in time. You guys are really lucky," he says again. "One thing, though. You really should have taken your friend to the hospital when you got out. There's this thing that can happen called secondary drowning. You get a person out of the water, safe on shore. They're standing right in front of you, telling you they're fine. You see them breathing, talking, then ten minutes later they're dead. Drowned from the water they still had in their lungs. The salt pulls even more liquid in. Yeah, you shoulda got your friend to the hospital."

I tell Leah what the lifeguard has said, ask her if she can remember anything else. "I remember the rock," she says. "And then I remember you yelling at me to crawl. I guess I did lose consciousness out there. I just remember at one point that everything started looking so incredibly beautiful." She drifts off. Returns. "The blues were amazing. Every time I got pulled under I just looked for where the blues got translucent, almost silvery white. That's how I knew where to swim up for air. Then I remember one time when I looked and everything was this radiant indigo color that pulsated aqua. It was so beautiful, like I was wrapped up in a silver blanket, resting in this soft blue bed. I felt my mind far, far off wonder if I was maybe dying, but the thought had no emotion in it." She turns to me, her eyes all soft, excited. "Do you think that was what it was like when my mom drowned? I always thought it must have been so horrible. Maybe it was beautiful. Maybe she saw what I saw."

Every memory Leah has, every insight, is one of beauty, strength, hope. Her friends tell her she has never been so radiant. "I'm in love," she exclaims, grabbing my arm. "Of course I'm radiant. I have my life, my very own life. The sea took me in and gave me such gifts. I am writing again. I've quit therapy. My heart is so open, so full. I feel so alive."

I am not in love, although I still hold her close to me at night. My dreams are getting worse. Drowning, going under, losing my grip, flashes of David's face rising up out of the coffin. I dream a recurring nightmare I haven't had for years. As a child I was always an animal in my dreams. The monsters were human. In this dream I am a young cougar, sometimes a wolf. I am running in the woods, not away from anything, not toward anything, just running hard. I feel the strength of my chest, my shoulders, my legs pounding across the ground. Grass slaps against my face. My nostrils flare to take in air, to take in scent. As I'm running I become aware of a hunter, his rifle pointed at me, fixing me in its sights. I feel the red cross-marks move across my body, settling on my right shoulder. I know I am about to be shot. I think about running faster, darting away, hiding behind the trees. But I just keep running, feeling my body, feeling my strength. Then I hear an explosion and my shoulder rips open. I run a few more strides in slow motion and then crash to the ground. I feel the hot bullet splinter my bones, tear through my flesh. Night after night I fight to keep from drowning. Night after night I run through the woods, knowing I'll be shot, keeping my stride until the bullet comes.

I am still coughing. A chest X-ray shows fluid in my lungs. The doctor gives me antibiotics. A healer friend lays her hands on me each week. "Please get the ocean out of my body," I plead. "I feel like there are fish swimming in my lungs." She eases the clenching in my throat, soothes the tightness around my chest. I weep when she places her hands on what she calls my heart chakra.

"I can help you with the fluid in your lungs," she says. "And I can help with the tissue damage in your throat and bronchioles. But you are drowning in your grief. Maybe you need to cry more," she tells me. She makes me promise her I will not take my life.

"What are you talking about?" I say. "I've never been suicidal. I feel like I am fighting *for* my life."

"You are," she says, looking older than I remember her.

I don't know how to cry any more than I already am. I don't know where all this water is coming from. I cannot drive. I cannot work. Some days I find myself in front of the TV at five p.m. watching *Baywatch,* watching *Rescue 911.* Every time I choke at the sight of the ocean, sob through the Technicolor rescues, the bobbing heads, the weeping loved ones on shore, clutching one another. I don't know who I am anymore, I tell whoever will listen. I feel like I am dying.

"You are having a spiritual breakthrough," friends tell me. "You are so lucky to have this opportunity to leave the past behind, to split away from your ego."

"I'm not having a spiritual breakthrough," I say. "I'm watching fucking *Baywatch.*"

The healer works on my lungs, relaxing the tight grip in my chest. I lay back into her soft burgundy blanket. "You need to start trying to breathe deeper," she says. "Try to pull the air all the way into your body. Feel it move through you."

"I need to start working out again," I tell her. "I hate being this fucking weak. I hate it that the ocean just pulled me backward like I was a little piece of nothing when I was swimming with all my strength."

The healer laughs, gently touching my cheek. "You're the strongest woman I've ever known," she says. "Don't you get it? Arnold Schwarzenegger in his prime couldn't have done squat out there in that ocean. This is not about physical strength." She places one hand under my back and the other over my heart. "Just try and breathe now," she says. "Relax. Let me know if this gets to be too much."

I relax into the warmth of the soft blanket, easing into the familiar heat and touch of her hands. I feel very young. She seems extraordinarily kind. The pressure on my chest increases and I try to breathe into it without coughing. Then it becomes too much and I try to tell her my chest is being crushed but I cannot speak and I open my eyes to see her hand still hovering just above my breastbone, not even touching me and then

I am in the emergency room, strapped down on a gurney. I am twenty-two years old. I have just totaled my car in a head-on crash on Carmel Valley Road delivering newspapers. I am fine, but they are wheeling me down the corridor, heading toward the X-ray room. I need to get back to work, finish the route. The X-ray technicians lift me into position, taking a front, rear, and two side views of my chest. A purple bruise gathers where I hit the steering wheel and I wait for them to develop the film so I can be released. I hear the technicians in the other room. "Jesus Christ," one of them says. "Look at this. She must have broken every single bone in her body. I've never seen anything like this before. Look at all these bone scars." Another voice, a woman, says, "I'll talk with her."

The older nurse comes back into the room, avoiding my eyes, setting up the X-rays on the lighted view case on the far wall. She raises up the back of my gurney so I can see. "Well," she begins, "it's not too bad. You do have three fairly significant fractures." She points. "Here, here, and here." I see three dark crevices running through the bright, white ribs on the screen. "That's why it is kind of hard for you to breathe right now," she tells me. "There's not really much to be done. I'll wrap them, but mostly you just need to take it easy and they will heal on their own."

"Okay," I say. "Can I get dressed and go?" I hate hospitals.

She looks over at me, frowning. "That must have been a really awful accident you were in," she says.

"Aw, it wasn't that bad," I say. "See, just a few busted ribs." I start to get up.

"No, I mean when you were a child," she says.

"I wasn't in an accident as a child," I tell her.

She points her stick back up to the screen, tracing tiny, pale lines running through nearly all my ribs. "See all these places where there are the faint, grey lines?" she asks. "Every one of these is a scar from where your ribs have been broken. I assumed it must have been an accident when you were very young."

I shrug, looking toward the door. "I don't know," I tell her. "I never was in an accident. I fell out of a tree once, wrecked my bike, got in some fights, that kind of stuff. Shit happens when you're a kid. You know. Can I get dressed now?" I ask again. I don't remember anything about my childhood before the age of five. I want to leave, get out quickly before her pity suffocates me.

"That's right, honey, just let it go. Just cry. That's really good."

I open my eyes to see the healer looking down at me, her eyes soft. I didn't know that I was crying. My face is wet. I shiver and she pulls the blanket closer around my shoulders. "You've been gone quite a while," she says. I tell her about the emergency room, the fractured ribs, the baby, ghostlike scars. She listens carefully, nodding. "Bones never lie," she says. "Your body remembers everything."

I turn away, pulling my knees up to my chest, rocking myself. It shocks me to think that my body remembers something I don't. "I've always been able to count on my body," I tell her. "It's my body, my strength, my ability to run, to fight, that's kept me alive."

The healer puts her hand on my shoulder. Softly, she says: "Yes, and your body remembers all the times you could *not* run."

Back home the ranch looks different. I can't find my dog. I call, whistle for her, suddenly afraid she has been killed or injured. She is so old. I want to feel her fur, tousle her ears, wrestle with her like before, hide her blue rubber ball and watch her retriever body spring into action. Practically deaf, half blind, still she has the fierce nose of a bird dog and the eager heart of a puppy. I finally spot her way over on the far ridge of the Brehmer Ranch, trotting like a coyote. She shouldn't be that far away. Everything feels strange, different. My cat follows close to me, watching with full feline attention, but skittish, running when I turn toward her. Only the horses have stayed the same. I pull the burrs from their tails, brush their manes, curry them for hours until I'm dripping wet and their coats shine, glossy in the sun. While I brush the dark bay mare, the chestnut gelding pushes gently into my shoulder, pulls the hoof pick out of my back pocket, mouths my hair, blowing warm, sweet breath into my neck. He lets me stretch out on his back as he eats his evening hay. Both their bodies feel strong, warm, solid. Familiar. Everything else has changed.

"You're just afraid of falling in love," says Leah. "I know. It scares me, too. But it's so good what we have."

"But *we* don't have anything," I say. "*You* have an idea about us. You have an idea of who you need me to be for you. Okay, maybe I saved your life. But now I'm not even here. Don't you get it? Everything I was, everything I had, everything I understood got washed out to sea. Even my fucking Levi jacket with my last sixty bucks in it. Okay? There is no 'me' here anymore to be 'in love' with you."

"Maybe my dad will give you some reward money for saving my life when he comes out to California," Leah says. "Don't worry. It will all be okay. I know I'm not in this alone and I know I'm not making it up. This love is way too good. My life is way too good."

Every night the dreams come. The drowning dreams. The getting shot dreams. One night a vision comes to me. I can't tell if it is an old man or woman, but it is a very wrinkled elder who smells like sage and sweat and forest. The elder puts one hand on my back and one on my heart, barely touching, and I feel the heat. There are no words, yet I clearly hear the thought: *Remember, if you are ocean you cannot drown.*

I wonder who is talking and how they know what I have never told anyone, that every day I find peace in a daydream, that the only time my throat unclenches is when I imagine myself driving down the coast in my red truck. I drive slow, watching for critters running out on the road, looking at the incredible beauty of the coastline. I pull off on the gravel turnout for Garrapata Beach, park the truck, and carefully hike down the cliff. On the beach, I begin to take off all my clothes, slowly. There is a slight breeze and the air feels cool. Naked, I open my arms to the sun, arching my back, breathing deeply. Then I walk into the surf, my heart liquid, bursting with joy. Surrender.

Giving Thanks

Any work whose journey has spanned more than a decade is bound to have an extensive band of gratitude recipients, and the folks who have believed in and supported these unruly characters along the way are bountiful and impressive.

I give thanks to Ann Todd Jealous, Bettina Aptheker, and Kate Miller for first championing these girls and believing their stories needed to be heard. Big gratitude to UCSC folks Roz Spafford, for wise support, and Carla Frecerro, for framing stories as narratives of resistance; to Mills crew Elmaz Abinader, Ginu Kamani, Toi Derricotte, Julie Shigekuni, Micheline Marcom, and Kim Hall for having my back every step of the way; to June Jordan for refusing to surrender; and Lucille Clifton, whose early support of Jackson and belief that linear time-defying ancestor truths are as real as any others kept me grounded and the work affirmed.

Deep gratitude to my lovely comrades at CSU Monterey Bay and the Creative Writing and Social Action Program: Frances Payne Adler ("Deb, you gotta get that book out there!"), Diana Garcia, Pam Motoike, Annette March, Maria Villasenor, Rina Benmayor, Ernie Stromberg, Umi Vaughan, and two amazing students, Nicole Jones and Monica Murdock, who first taught some of these stories in the Women's Writing Workshop with such brilliance, grace, and expertise I almost wept with joy.

Appreciation for all the books and journals that have published parts of this novel in various forms: Eleven Eleven: A Journal of Literature and Art, Issue 15, 2013; Street Lit: Representing the Urban Landscape, 2014; Combined Destinies: Whites Share Grief About Racism, 2013; Fire & Ink: An Anthology of Social Justice Writing, 2009; and The Los Angeles Review: Number 4 – 2007.

Special thanks to Laurie Stapleton and Susan McCloskey, who "got" and affirmed this book at especially critical junctures; to Faith Adiele for a most timely encounter in the literary woods of Hedgebrook. Grateful to be blessed with the most supportive family one could dream of, and for Akasha Gloria Hull and Dana McRae, who had to live and/or hang with me during important chunks of the book's journey and who still loved and supported me anyway, cheering on these wild girls and their beleaguered writer every step of the way.

Huge appreciation to my incredible agent Dana Newman and the terrific crew at Dzanc Books, whose love for literature and joyful perseverance in publishing is a most beautiful thing to behold. Michelle Dotter's keen editorial eye and structural expertise has been especially astute and delightful. I feel so honored and fortunate to have such great folks shepherding this book along the way, making all this possible.

And, always, deep gratitude to all the four-leggeds—Bucky, J. Edgar, Jai, Shen, Kai, Coco, Sar, Xena, Uma, Cayla, and Luca— great beings who have taught me love and kept me in this world, sustaining spirit and giving heart for the journey.

I dedicate this book to all the kids and teens, queer and allies, who have and are currently living on the streets, making a way out of no way to find love and forge survival and resistance.